A Heart Beats Within

THE STORY OF A ROCKING HORSE

LANA GAZDER

First published in Great Britain as a softback original in 2021

Copyright © Lana Gazder

The moral right of this author has been asserted.

All characters and events in this publication, other than those clearly in the public domain, are fictitious and any resemblance to real persons, living or dead, is purely coincidental.

All rights reserved.

No part of this publication may be reproduced, stored in a retrieval system, or transmitted, in any form or by any means, without the prior permission in writing of the publisher, nor be otherwise circulated in any form of binding or cover other than that in which it is published and without a similar condition including this condition being imposed on the subsequent purchaser.

Illustrations © Lana Gazder

Cover illustration: © Theresa Delacey Vallecarde

Editing, design, typesetting and publishing by UK Book Publishing
www.ukbookpublishing.com

Typeset in Dante MT Std

ISBN: 978-1-914195-54-9

This book is dedicated with thanks to *Helen Robbins* for her inspiration, help and support.

Also, to *Tim* and *Jacqueline* for making it all possible.

A Heart Beats Within

CHAPTER 1. 'NO.7'

"Strong winds make for strong trees"

I have had many names during my life, but I started out as just plain 'No. 7'. Perhaps I should explain: I'm not a real live flesh and blood horse but a sculpted horse made of wood. I am a rocking horse. However, I am alive and have a heart that beats within my wooden body and I have lived a long and eventful life. There is no doubt that I am extremely beautiful and rather special. Because I was created with so much realism, love and care, somehow my wooden body came to life. It's hard to explain but I will try and start at the beginning.

I came into this world a long time ago, when Queen Victoria was an old lady coming to the end of her reign and rocking horses were all the rage for young children of well-to-do families. We were bought to live in the nurseries of huge mansions and country houses. Although we were basically toys, we were also important to help teach young children how to ride. We provided a way for them to learn balance during movement, to have a deep and secure seat and kind hands. An important rule was for hands to be held low at all times to avoid hurting our delicate mouths.

Youngsters adored us; we were their pride and joy. They would sit astride us on our luxurious hand-made saddles, rocking crazily as if in a gallop and imagine they were out in the hunting field or on the race-course. They mimicked their parents, whose beautiful blood horses of high mettle lived in the mansions' stables and were taken out on daily rides to grace the countryside. Compared to the shabby work cobs or heavy farm horses of the local people, those steeds were the envy of the less fortunate. We, as spirited rocking horses, made the poorer children who may have only had plain hobby-horses, look upon us with wistful eyes.

Within the confines of the nursery, rocking horses didn't always have a life of leisure. If we were ridden too hard we could be driven forward to cause our heads and ears to smash into furniture or walls. Sometimes if we were mounted carelessly, this could make us tip over to crash awkwardly on our sides. Accidents did happen, especially with over-enthusiastic boys who rode as if being chased by the devil, rocking too high and fast. Little girls tended to ride more gently especially as they had to practise riding in the side-saddle fashion. I found girls often preferred to stroke us, whisper their secrets into our pricked ears, play with our flowing manes and simply hug us whilst riding at a sedate rock. The main job of the nursery horse was to keep the family's children occupied and content, to be a friend they could talk to and a toy to fire their imagination.

1899. This is the year that I was born. Well maybe not exactly born, perhaps created is a better description of the long process I had to undergo to come to life. Many trees were felled to give me and others of my kind our form. The wood used to make us had to be carefully dried out and only when it was well 'seasoned' could we be safely hewn without fear of us warping or cracking when we were finished. Each horse was made up of many pieces or blocks of wood to be fashioned into our horse form. Our bodies were basically a hollow box made of one wood, usually yellow pine. Our legs were carved from another stronger hardwood such as beech, as legs support the whole body and come under tremendous strain when we are rocked with weight on our backs. Good toy makers always used the best timber available. Good timber made strong horses that could last for ever...

"A thing of beauty is a joy forever."
– John Keats.

I started life in a small family-owned workshop in the middle of London. The firm's owner was called Mr Paul Leach. My Maker, who was one of a few men who worked for Mr Leach, was a kind and talented carpenter who had a daughter called Florence who also laboured in the rocking horse factory. She was an expert painter and would decorate our bodies and give us our manes and tails near the end of our manufacture. There were lots of big firms busy making rocking horses all over the country, but mostly in London and some were hugely famous. Even our dear Queen Victoria visited a workshop to buy one of us for her children! Apparently she chose a dappled grey horse, giving that colour her Royal seal of approval. That's how loved we were by our nation, how important we were to our country's children and I'm so proud to be what I am.

Mr Leach's shop was small in comparison to some, but he had a wonderful reputation for producing beautifully shaped, realistic horses of great quality. He employed workers who loved horses, true artists, who knew every muscle and sinew on the real animal and put that extra detail into their carving. My memories are rather vague as I was so young at the start of my making process, but I do remember being one of several horses balanced on a work-bench in a line with others like me. Here I was known as No.7. My Maker talked to me as he chiselled away, forming my shapely body and elegant head. As he worked on my ears, I found I could hear his every word and the general friendly chatter of the workers around me. When he chiselled out my trumpet-like flared nostrils, I realised I could pick up various smells in the air, mainly the aromatic scent of fresh pinewood being worked. Once we were carved into a horse shape, we had to be filed down, a job that prepared us for our next stage.

I'm not sure when I realised I was different to the other horses around me, as the process happened gradually. Perhaps it was what I heard my Maker say every day he worked on me. He would mutter under his breath, "No.7, me lad, you're one of a kind, you are." Or he would declare, "I can't fathom it, your wood feels so warm to touch. Bless me, you could be a real livin' horse!" If he saw his daughter, he'd pull her over to admire me. "Pa, you'll get me into trouble, keepin' me away from me paintin." He'd say, "But Flo, juss look at him! He's summat special is my No.7. There's just summat about him. I needs him to go to a real

La-di-da home where he'll be treasured." Even his wife heard stories about me. She dropped off my Maker's lunch one day and approached me in mock awe, whispering, "So this here's the famous No. 7? The one you say you hear a heart a thumpin' in his chest when you sand him down? Well, I have to tell you, Wilf, he's a beaut an' no mistake, but p'raps you should lay off the ale a bit, you silly ole fool!"

When my shaping was complete and I'd been meticulously filed and rounded off, I was given my beautiful big brown glass eyes. This is when I truly felt I had come to life. All my senses were awakened and I was aware of going through the stage of having my 'gesso' applied. Gessoing is the process that makes us smooth and ready for painting. Oh, the aroma was awful as it was made of a chalky white powder mixed to a paste with smelly rabbit glue. This was painted on me while it was still warm (which was very pleasant, I have to admit) in several coats over several days. When I was fairly dry, I was taken to be stored 'in the white'. My six brothers and I were carefully carried to an airy barn so our newly-applied gesso could really set and 'cure'. The weeks I spent there were a bit lonely as the other horses didn't seem able to see or hear, so I couldn't talk to them. When we returned from drying, another long and arduous task began. Our gesso was carefully rubbed down to prepare us for painting. This was a painstaking job that took a measure of patience and skill. I really enjoyed this process as it felt so good, except for the clouds of dust!

My Maker came over to admire me when I was sanded to a smooth finish. He ran his cupped hand over my newly white arched neck and laid his palm on my chest to check he hadn't been mistaken about the beating heart he had heard whilst working on me. He looked deep into my eyes and promised he'd get Florence to paint me and apply my harness, as she was the best in the business. He told me I would soon be off to my first home; a very grand family had ordered me for their son's Christmas present. "Don't worry. It's a La-di-da home, what you deserve, lad."

"Pride comes before a fall."

Florence did a wonderful job of decorating me. With care and patience, she painted me deftly and with great skill. She dappled my whole body with feather-like brush strokes and as she delicately painted my spidery eyelashes, she told me my eyes were a window to my soul. Crimson paint was applied to the insides of my ears, my flared nostrils and the detail of my tongue and mouth. To finish me off, Florence gave me my crowning glory, a wonderful horse-hair mane and forelock which cascaded down between my pricked ears and curved neck. She attached a tail to my sleek quarters which flowed majestically over my smokey- black hocks to trail into my new stand. Yes, I was a modern horse graced with a carved wooden swing stand.

Our original way of being attached to two large bow rockers had become thought of as a little unsafe and before I was born, a new design for a rocking stand was invented. This swinging stand took up less room and did no damage to wooden floors. Also, WE were less likely to be hurt and little human toes were less likely to be crushed under heavy rockers. By the time I was made, parents could choose whether to buy a horse on bows or swing stands. I was thought to be very up-to-date and deserved to be mounted on a stand.

Once my paint and varnish had dried to a soft sheen, Florence gave me a thick velvet saddle cloth to wear on my back. It was edged with gold tassels which glinted and shimmered every time I was moved. My saddle and bridle were fitted next, using shiny brass studs. My bridle was adorned with silk rosettes, one either side of my face and a third one, worn on my chest. The smell of that new leather was intoxicating. I can't describe how smart I felt now I was complete and ready to start a new life. When Florence was satisfied with the finishing touches, she called her father over to inspect her work. He was delighted and his eyes shone with pride as he whispered, "You're me best one yet. Don't forget, lad, you're special." He wished me a long and happy life and told me to be kind to all the children who rode me. That was the final time I saw my lovely Maker.

The day came, close to Christmas, when I was polished and ready to go. I was known as a Traditional English Dapple Grey rocking horse. I was carved in the elegant form of a well-bred hack, with head held in the 'collected' position. This indicated I was spirited but well-mannered enough for a child to ride me in the side-saddle style. As all rocking horses of the best quality, my head and neck had that elegant 'turn' to the off-side and furthermore I wore the most expensive tack attached to me with the prettiest decorative studs in the shop.

They placed me in the front of the shop on display and being luckier than most, I sported a 'RESERVED' label. Already feeling quite important, I then caught a glimpse of my reflection in the show-room window and was delighted. I had a lot to learn. Over many years I have found that pride can be a dangerous thing. Don't they say pride comes before a fall? Admittedly, being a very proud youngster in those early days, I swelled with self-importance at seeing my image, those beautiful glass eyes, the dapples, my prancing outline and flowing mane. But this pride was pure vanity and that's not a good thing. Now, as a wise old horse, I have learned it's alright to feel pride as long as you are humble with it.

Chapter 2 'Blizzard'

"Embrace change; it helps us to grow."

The Christmas of 1899 came in like a lion. Strong biting winds blew the snow this way and that. There was an air of excitement as daylight broke, and my brothers and I were loaded into carts to be delivered to our new homes. We were destined as Christmas presents for our lucky children. Wrapped up snuggly in thick grey blankets, I was carefully lifted onto a cart and heard the muffled instructions shouted to my driver. "This 'un's for that big house in Chiswick, Kilwick Manor. Don't take all day, there's lots more to go out…"

Being so vain in those early days, all I could think about was how much my mane was being rubbed and tangled by the cumbersome blankets. I felt every bump in the road and it took an age to get there. At last the ruts gave way to a smooth long drive and we headed to the back of Kilwick Manor where the servants and a Butler were awaiting my arrival. With hushed whispers, they carried me up many stairs, up to the very top of my new home – a huge attic nursery. One of the blankets had slipped off my face, so I had seen everything since arriving. Yes, it certainly was a 'La-di-da' residence! And joy of joys, I'm sure I saw another one of my sort, a very refined, pretty grey rocking horse on huge bows. He was in the opposite corner, looking surprised and pleased to see me.

The slipped blanket was replaced to hide my head and the staff scurried off to fetch my eight year old owner. I was his Christmas surprise! People approached and I heard the Nanny's voice clearly as she declared, "There you are, Master Augustus, your present from Mater and Pater. Go and see then!" Heavy footsteps thumped towards me, several rough tugs stripped me of my blankets and as they fell to the floor, I was revealed in all my glory. A rather scowling young face looked at me critically. My new boy, who was affectionately called Gus, walked around my stand inspecting every detail of my fine body. He callously prodded and pushed hard on my neck to test my swinging action. At last a sneaky smile spread across his coarse features as he gave his verdict to an expectant audience. "I say, what a cracking good steed this is. I bet he'll go a fair lickety-spit gallop for me, heh, Sis?"

What a sweet little child his sister was in comparison to her heavy-set brother. She was dainty; perhaps even a touch mousy, but radiated kindness and goodwill. He continued in a cruel and teasing tone. "I'll be giving you a thrashing when we next race. Your silly little Cobweb is so slow, he's only fit for the glue factory!" His Nanny rebuked him for this unkind remark, but he shrugged it off with a toss of his dark hair and as he left the room he declared, "I'll name him Blizzard! He arrived in a filthy snowstorm and he's going to go like the wind!" His lovely little sister Gracie ran to me and kissed my nose gently, whispering, "Well, Blizzard, I think you're gorgeous and I hope you make friends with my darling lonely Cobweb. I'm sorry you'll have Gus riding you. He broke his last horse, you know..."

"People who fly into a rage always make a bad landing." – **Anonymous.**

My first week at Kilwick Manor soon passed, during which I had to learn quickly how to cope with my situation and how to survive. I seemed to have started my career with a rather angry and bullying young owner. Perhaps it was bad luck but then I've learned over the years that you must make your own luck. I tried to do as my Maker had bid me – be kind to the children who rode me – but this proved hard with Augustus. All he wanted to do was be like his father who rode recklessly in point-to-points and steeplechases. At first, I was quite a novelty and he wanted to ride me daily. I had to tolerate his awful way of mounting me, un-balancing me sideways, then thumping down heavily in the saddle. He would push me roughly into a terrifyingly fast pace until my beech legs creaked under the strain. His hands were never still; they jiggled and ripped at my mouth as he leapt over hedge and ditch in his mind's eye.

I now realise that my wonderful looks were actually working against me. If I had been plain and ordinary, perhaps Gus wouldn't have paid me so much attention. But like his father, he had a good eye for a horse and it was my beauty that had attracted him. So, during that first week I endured being ridden hard with no thought or care – that was until my first real 'accident', after which I learned a clever rocking horse trick!

Near the end of that first week, Gus roped his poor little sister into a fearful race between me and Cobweb. The little grey horse and I had become firm friends, quietly chatting together when alone in the nursery. Cobweb was older than me and was a delicately built rocking horse made by the famous firm of G&J Lines. With a wonderfully dappled body like mine, he wore the Thistle badge of his maker on his chest to prove his high quality. This clever little horse taught me that we could swing our weight about secretly to move ourselves around the attic. We would stand shoulder to shoulder and gaze from the small attic window on to the magnificent view of Kilwick Manor grounds. Cobweb told me many stories. He explained that not many of us rocking horses could speak, so he was delighted when I had come to live with him. We didn't talk aloud in actual words, it was more of a transfer of thoughts and feelings, but it worked beautifully and made us completely content. After our chats, we would shuffle away to different corners before the maids came to dust the room. As we were moveable anyway, no one ever suspected a thing as we were often shifted about for the floor to be swept and the rugs to be beaten.

Now let me tell you about that awful day when we were made to race against each other. It wasn't a race of moving speed, more of violent action with a lot of whip-brandishing and taunting cries. Gus would drag us into position side by side to start the fictitious race. This day he had misjudged our placing and we were straddled halfway upon a slippery rug. Poor little Gracie looked terrified, bullied into riding Cobweb side saddle whilst Gus barked at her to ride faster and higher. I was dangerously near a chest of drawers and with every shuddering push from the saddle, Gus inched me closer to the furniture. My stand slipped on the loose rug, crashing my poor head against the top drawer of the chest. With a roar of delight, Gus proclaimed that he was the victor. Gracie was sobbing with pity for me as she could see my shapely ear was split and a splinter of crimson wood hung down, attached by a thin sliver. The chest had also suffered a loss. One of the wooden drawer knobs had been flung to the floor where it landed and spun around in a small circle. A horrible silence was soon broken with the unrepentant boy muttering, "Oh well, injuries are all part of racing. Too bad!" Gus wrenched and twisted off my loose chunk of ear, picked up the wooden knob and looked round the room trying to decide where best to hide the evidence of his crime. Then a sly smile spread across his face and he tore at my saddle flap to reveal my pommel hole. Here he stuffed the ear splinter and the round wooden knob. They fell with a dull thud into the depths of my belly. Holding his whip up above his head, he turned on Gracie with a vile threat. "If you dare breathe a word, I'll come back and give Cobweb a good hiding!"

Oh, I forgot to tell you about my secret hidey-hole. Most of us are made with these holes into which our side saddle-pommels are attached. These 'pommel' appendages help keep small riders secure by allowing them to hook a leg around for extra purchase. When I first arrived, Augustus had angrily removed the pommels and thrown them into the toy box. He declared that they were only fit for sissies and no silly girls would be riding Blizzard if he had his way. Even in those early days, I was a good judge of character. My first impressions of both children were correct. I knew my life would be miserable being owned by this petulant youth, who had the potential to do me real damage. I was young and strong and made of the best wood, but nevertheless, I did not relish a repeat of that ugly incident in the nursery.

"When life gets hard to endure, a solution is the only cure."

I certainly had a big problem; my vanity was fading fast with every small injury and abusive kick and jab I received from my angry young rider. Although still proud, I was humble enough to seek help from Cobweb, who had sadly watched the outcome of that fateful race. I asked for advice and was told of a clever idea that might just save my life. Gus had a nasty habit of stomping heavily on the back of Cobweb's bows whilst Gracie was on board. This terrified her as she would end up rocking dangerously high and fast. So Cobweb had devised a method of keeping his beloved Gracie safe. If she was rocking too high, he would throw his weight in the opposite direction, slowing up his motion. As Gracie was so small, he could also push his weight forwards to help her if she was struggling to start rocking. This method, which he called the 'reverse-weight trick', allowed him to assist her and keep her from harm. I gave an approving nod. I would start practising and employ this clever ruse the next time I was at risk.

My chance came the very next day. After trial and error, I perfected the trick so well that young Gus slouched off me in disgust after failing to attain his normal reckless speed. Aiming his usual hateful kick at my hocks, he sneered and muttered, "Huh, you didn't take long to turn into a sluggish nag! I'll get that gardener chap to oil your metal bits. No good looking flash if you can't go a gallop…" So I had to pretend to improve after the unnecessary greasing and decided to only employ the trick when it was vital.

Now I have given you an impression of my time at Kilwick Manor, I'm sad to report that things continued in a similar vein for a few years. During this time, I began to understand why Gus behaved as he did, and I actually felt sorry for the child. He was only copying the behaviour of his father who had set him a horrible example all his young life. This was highlighted when Cobweb and I witnessed a shocking sight as we gazed out of the nursery window one autumn morning. Gus and his father were on the lawn below, as the groom led out a sturdy hunter who looked rather lame. "I'm afraid you won't be able to ride him today, Sir. He has a filled tendon and is very sore." Gus looked up at his father's face to see his reaction. We were horrified to hear his father retort angrily, "Don't be ridiculous, lad! Tack him up NOW. Put a tight bandage on that leg and bring him back, quick as you like. We don't keep shirkers in THIS yard!" There is no happy ending to this story as the poor horse returned hours later, hobbling on three legs. Later that day we both heard it: the unmistakable loud crack of a gun.

After tea, when the children came in to play and have their usual ride on us, I noticed Gracie was quite distraught. Instead of swaying contentedly upon Cobweb's back, happily humming in her usual way, she just clung on with arms around his neck, sobbing loudly into his mane until it was quite damp. Even Gus was subdued but he showed his mood in his usual cruel manner. "Stop that infernal crying. It was only a horse. If you don't stop snivelling, I'll give you something to weep about…I'll beat Cobweb with a stick 'till his dapples fall off!" Nanny sent Gus off to bed as a punishment for his bad behaviour, but not before he'd given me another well-aimed kick in my leg on his way out.

My life at Kilwick was thankfully coming to an end. On his 12th birthday, Augustus received a present from his father which happily made me redundant. He was given a real pony, a well-built black Welsh cob. I couldn't help feeling sorry for the poor thing but utterly relieved for myself! I stood idle for a while and enjoyed the peaceful atmosphere that reigned over the attic. Gracie's school friends, who lived in the local Rectory, came often and played with us horses, grooming our manes and tails carefully with an old dog brush. One afternoon they decided to try me out and one by one, clambered quite gently into my saddle. I was extremely careful to give them all a lovely ride. I made the most of that wonderful feeling of being appreciated. Those children grew to adore me as much as Gracie loved Cobweb. I wished I could feel this newfound happiness for a while longer…

Well, my wish came true. Gus' father, who didn't tolerate 'shirkers' even in the nursery, decided to get rid of me, for a price. The Rector had been nagged and harassed by his brood of six children to buy them a rocking horse. I suppose it was my fault. They had just fallen in love with me while visiting Gracie. Now they wished for their own rocking horse. Their mother would say, "If wishes were horses then beggars would ride, love." Annie, the youngest of the siblings, replied, "What ever does THAT mean?" Her elder brother replied with a hollow laugh, "It means we are not rich enough to have a posh toy horse, so stop wishing. We haven't the money." The Rector was a gentle, kindly man and all he wanted was to make his children happy. But rocking horses like us were so expensive; he knew he could never afford to buy a brand new one. After weeks of hearing about Blizzie wasting away in the Kilwick attic, an idea struck him.

He headed off the very next day to try and buy me for his children. He met with Gus' father and was taken to view us in the old nursery. When he first saw my beauty and splendour, he was somewhat taken aback, but hid it well. A huge price was being asked, but the Rector was a knowledgeable horseman and a canny buyer. He inspected me carefully with a poker face, as one would when buying a horse from the market. The Rector said in a very calm voice, "I'm afraid this horse has quite a bit of damage on it, weakening its structure and ruining its appearance. It has big dents and crumbling gesso on its legs and half its ear is missing." Gus' father was furious and summoned his son to explain my wounds. "That horse cost me a great deal of money! How the devil did you do all this damage to it?" Gus showed no guilt at his bare-faced lie as he squarely blamed the poor housemaids for being clumsy. By now his father was annoyed and too busy to waste time quibbling over a mere few shillings. He accepted the Rector's rather low offer, just to be rid of the whole irritating matter.

So this was farewell to Kilwick Manor after four years of calling it home. My delivery to the Rectory was arranged for the very next day, hardly time to say goodbye to my friends. I know I'm only made of wood, but for the first time in my life I felt awfully sad to be leaving Gracie and dear Cobweb. Never before had I had this strange sensation, but the corners of my glass eyes felt quite damp.

CHAPTER 3 'SONATA'

"The supreme happiness of life is the conviction that we are loved." – **Victor Hugo.**

1904

I was now a four year old, a mere youngster in rocking horse terms. My first home had taught me that money does not always buy happiness and good looks don't always work in your favour. My new life at the Rectory proved to be quite joyful. Looking back, it was one of the happiest homes of my career. What made this place so different? I think it was because this house was bursting with warmth and love. At Kilwick Manor, despite all the roaring fires, the house had felt icy cold. Here at the Rectory, it was untidy in a comfortable, homely way and full of the sound of laughing children. The rector's wife, Mrs Tubb, was often in the kitchen and the delicious aroma of baking would waft through to my nostrils. This is where I developed my love of classical music because the Rector adored the composer J. S. Bach. He had been lucky enough to acquire an amazing machine, a gramophone, from one of his parishioners. This wealthy banker had emigrated to America, leaving the machine in the care of the Rector. Strains of Bach's wonderful compositions could be heard all day long. It was just so wonderful to be in the centre of so much life.

I clearly remember the day I was delivered to the Rectory. The children shrieked with excitement at my arrival and followed me into the house, thrilled at their luck and the clever way I had been obtained from the grand Manor. Instead of being shipped off to the furthest room in the house, the family hurriedly cleared a space for me on the floor of the sprawling parlour. Here I stayed, right in the middle of all that glorious activity, where I could see and hear every bit of family life. I was still a very grand horse, still imposingly magnificent. On that first day, the children sat round me for a long time, just gazing. They soon got used to my presence and I quickly felt part of my new family. The youngest three girls fussed over me, brushing and kissing me as they had when visiting Kilwick. Annie was the most besotted; she never left my side. She often sat against my stand rail, playing with toys but with her pudgy little arm linked through one of my legs. The smaller ones couldn't reach my saddle, but Tom or Albert, their elder brothers, would kindly lift them aboard. Little Annie would rock me with glee and was quick to shout to her mother that she'd been wrong, and that beggars COULD ride! The girls would sit astride me chanting the ditty they'd learned from their brother. "If wishes were horses then beggars would ride, if turnips were swords, I'd have one by my side. If 'ifs' and 'ands' were pots and pans, there'd be no use for tinkers' hands!" It was just so lovely for me to feel useful and know I was being enjoyed by the children.

I'd been there a few weeks and noticed that no one ever called me by the name that Gus had given me. They didn't even call me Gracie's affectionate version of 'Blizzie'. Maybe they felt I'd not been happy at Kilwick and didn't want to be reminded of Gracie's vile brother! I was just referred to as 'Annie's horse'. Then, the Rector started to notice something strange about me. When he sat at his desk doing his clerical work, he could see me out of the corner of his eye. Whenever one of Bach's sonatas were playing, I couldn't help a feeling of serenity that came over me. Almost in a trance, I would sway gently with the music, unaware that I was even moving. But the Rector saw me on several occasions and at first, thought the breeze coming in through the open French windows was to blame. But then he began to wonder about me, gazing into my eyes and smiling warmly. I think he guessed I wasn't an ordinary rocking horse. He began to test me with doors shut and different music, but I only seemed to sway to sonatas. He told Mrs.Tubb his suspicions about my love of music and that I had something rather special about me. She dismissed his comments with a hearty laugh saying, "I'm too busy feeding, cleaning and running about after six young 'uns to have time to watch Annie's horse dancing to your blessed music! Yes, he is special; he keeps those children so happy and I'm more 'n grateful for that!" Anyway, after the music incident I was officially re-named 'Sonata' or just 'Sonny'. But nobody else really understood why...

My life now was all I ever hoped it would be. I felt useful and enjoyed my job of child-minding, almost like a Nanny! It was just a lovely household. The Rector had many needy parishioners or grieving parents come to visit. They came for comfort and solace. Mrs Tubb's cups of tea and fruit cake always helped and of course I was quite a talking point, the centrepiece of the room. I'm sure I brought them some joy for they never failed to comment on my beauty and grace, often bringing their youngsters back later to enjoy a quick ride on my back. And yes, I felt very proud. But I had changed; now I was proud that I could bring some pleasure and comfort to ease aching hearts.

Chapter 4 'Sonny'

"All men desire peace, but very few desire those things that make for peace." – **Thomas A Kempis.**

1914

At fourteen years old and still in possession of a thick flowing mane and tail, I felt extremely blessed. My family had treasured me and I had enjoyed ten happy years in my Rectory home, watching the delightful children growing up. I'm sure I would have remained with them as a valued and well-loved member of the family, but unfortunately times and circumstances change. Life is like that. Here I have to tell you of a dark and terrible time which was looming over the whole country. The Great War was about to break out. Why it was ever called that, I'll never fathom. It was a war that brought tragedy to so many families. Bombs fell. Men went to fight abroad in the most dreadful conditions and either never returned or came home badly damaged. Thousands upon thousands of lives were lost. Many animals died too. I heard from an old pony, a coal delivery cob, that so many horses were just taken away from their homes here in Britain and sent off to foreign countries to be ridden into battle or to pull heavy carts full of ammunition. I am told most of them never came home. A lot of rocking horses also died, shattered into pieces in the rubble of broken, bombed homes or burned with house timbers in the street. In fact, I only just escaped death by the skin of my dapples, but that part of my story will come later…

I listened to the Rector with a feeling of dread as he tried explaining to his family why their world had been turned upside down. By then Annie was fourteen (I always remember because we are the same age) but the eldest son, Tom, was now a young man. He wanted to be a soldier and fight for his country. The war may have started over something that happened far away, the assassination of some Austrian Archduke, but within a year we were in the thick of it, as the war came right to our doorstep in London.

"Courage is not the absence of fear; it is acting in spite of it." – **Mark Twain.**

1915 was the most terrifying summer I'd ever lived through. I and the whole family were living in constant fear of the unknown. The Germans flew huge monstrous airships called Zeppelins over our city. They came at night, blotting out all the stars with their dark shadows above us. Then the bombs rained down, spreading destruction and terror throughout London. Panic tore through every household. People ran to hide in underground tube stations.

Families huddled together in cellars and basements. I couldn't be taken to safety, so I stood near the parlour window and watched all the terrible things that happened out in the street. It was truly frightening and my heart felt frozen with fear.

There was worse news to come for me. I felt my family, who I thought loved me dearly, were deserting me. They were being relocated out of London to a country parish where bombs were less likely to fall. The beautiful happy Rectory home where I'd grown to feel so safe and contented, was about to be abandoned. I was feeling so fearful and confused until the family came to me one by one to explain what was happening. Annie and her siblings told me that they loved me and that I was like a brother to them. They promised they'd be back to live in the Rectory after the war and that I must stay safe till then. Kisses and hugs were showered upon me before they carried their trunks out to the waiting cab. Tom stroked my forelock and told me he was off to fight next week and he'd make sure we won the war and that we were all kept safe. Lastly the Rector came to me and looked into my eyes saying, "Sonny, how I wish I didn't have to leave you here but I need you to be brave and give as much joy as you can to the poor children who are coming to live here. This house is being turned into a shelter for those poor souls who have no parents. Do what you do best, Sonny, look after them." He turned on his heel and left and that was the last time I ever saw the Tubb family.

Perhaps if I were an ordinary wooden rocking horse without my heart, I would not have felt so terribly sad or scared. But then I would not have experienced love, laughter and joy or heard beautiful music, so perhaps it is worth feeling all those emotions that come with being alive. However, it would be a very long time before I heard any music again. After a few lonely days at the Rectory with no company, people started to arrive to make the house ready for the arrival of the orphaned children of the borough. My old home certainly changed. The aroma of baking bread was replaced with the overwhelming smell of boiled cabbage and thick oat gruel. The light airy rooms became gloomy as windows were sealed shut and blacked out for our safety. Bombs were less likely to fall on dark areas of the city, but everyone still lived in dread of those murderous night attacks.

Simple bunk beds were brought in and lined the walls of the parlour. I was moved to stand in front of the old French windows which used to be flung open in summer to allow the heady scent of jasmine and roses to waft in from the Rectory garden. Now they were obliterated by heavy drapes that smelled of dust and mould. A kindly lady known as Matron was fussing about making up the beds with threadbare sheets and heavy grey blankets. She glanced at me and said, "We'll leave Mr Handsome right here. I'm sure the younger ones would love to play with him." Another man, whom I recognised as the Church Warden and a good friend of Mr Tubb, said, "It was good of the family to leave him here. I'm sure he will be a comfort to those poor little mites. They've lost absolutely everything in their short lives. Most have no family left in the world. Apparently, his name is Sonny." After hearing that, I vowed to myself that no matter how scared I felt, I would try to comfort any child that came to me. I now realised the awful meaning of the word 'orphan'.

"Kind words can be short and easy to speak, but their echoes are truly endless." – **Mother Teresa.**

Oh, we all pulled together and worked so hard to make the Orphans' Refuge as homely and safe as we possibly could. The children arrived thick and fast, each bearing a tragic story of loss. Some were survivors of a bombed-out household where all their family had been killed. Brothers and sisters came clutching a few belongings that they had salvaged from their destroyed homes. Some were motherless children whose fathers had become soldiers and had then been killed on the battlefield. Matron lavished each one with love and care but in a matter of fact way, so as not to smother them. Food was basic and there was not really enough to go round. But the Warden often brought in home-grown fruit and vegetables, donated to the Orphanage by generous parishioners. A tin bath was regularly brought into the main room and filled from the kitchen's copper of hot water so each child could have a makeshift bath. Their faces and hands were scrubbed after each meal and they were dressed in ill-fitting but clean, warm hand-me-down clothes. There was always a kind word for a tearful child and a story told, to help the younger ones fall asleep at bedtime.

The children were instantly drawn to me and I'd never been so busy! Matron used me to encourage the difficult ones to behave by saying, "All the good little 'uns can have a play on Sonny!" Or, "No rocking on Sonny if you disobey...." I gave rides from dawn to dusk but I was always ridden gently and with respect. Admittedly, over-eager little hands caused some of my mane to be pulled out by mistake, but I never complained as I had stopped being vain about my appearance. I was just so happy to be giving some comfort to these sad little souls. Sometimes I had two or three sitting on me at once, but most were so slight of build, I hardly noticed their weight.

I learned much about their previous lives as they sat on and around me to play games and chat among themselves. One bright lad invented a pastime which entailed each child telling a story of a horse they'd known. Most talked fondly of their parents' work ponies or cobs. An older boy, Joe, told us about his much-loved chestnut van-horse 'Lemon Drizzle' who was owned by his father, the town's baker. The little lad had just learned how to drive him on his deliveries when the horse was snatched to go and fight in the war. Joe was sad but very proud that Drizzle was doing his war duty, as was his brave father. Joe's father lost his life fighting for his country.

There was one particular story of a horse that really stood out and fascinated me. It came from a brother and sister whom I had become extremely fond of. They were different to all the other children because they weren't really Londoners and they spoke in a secret language. They had the darkest eyes and hair as black as ebony. I had heard Matron talking to the Warden about them when everybody had gone to bed. Apparently, their parents had been killed many years before but their Uncle Jed had brought them up as if they were his own. They had moved from a place called the New Forest to London for him to seek work as a 'totter'. Totters were the people who went round with a pony and flat 'trolley' cart from house to house, collecting throwaway items such as old pots and pans, rags, broken iron objects and even old bones! They were also known as 'rag and bone men' and would go down the streets calling out "Rag-bone" or "Any old iron". People would appear at their front doors, arms laden with what they thought of as rubbish, because it seemed an easy way of disposing of it. The totter was a clever dealer and would sort out and recycle his day's takings to make a reasonable living.

Jed's niece and nephew were known in the Orphanage as Cindy and Fred. But I knew their real names, only spoken softly among themselves. Their birth names were Sinnaminti and Manfri (which is short for Manfred). Just through listening to their quiet conversations as they rocked me or sat by, I learned that they were actually Romany Gypsies. They were scared to let anyone know, because a lot of people showed discrimination towards gypsies. So they spoke their secret language in private and because I listened carefully to all that was said, I am proud to say I'm pretty good at understanding what they call Romany Jib (Gypsy tongue). Now I have explained who Sinni and Manfri really are, I'll get back to their story.

The children had gathered round me and most had told a tale of their favourite pony. All eyes turned to Cindy and Fred, who had remained silent up till then. The two looked at each other and smiled as they knew they had a cracking good story to tell. Fred, ever the showman and enjoying being the centre of attention, stood up ceremoniously and began the strange tale…

He said they had been accompanying their Uncle Jed on his rounds, picking up scrap metal from the factories behind the Grand Union canal. On their way home, their black and white cob pulled up sharply and peered through a hedge, where a deep stream ran through some scrubland. Nothing would convince the horse to move. He just dug his toes in until Jed leapt out of the cart to see what his horse has spotted. There, lying in the water, was a little roan-coloured pony, soaked to the skin and close to death. Nearby stood a mean looking stallion that it seemed had driven the little horse into the water to drown him. Jed saw a few bubbles coming from the pony's nostrils and guessed that although too exhausted to struggle any more, it was still alive. Moving swiftly, he grabbed ropes from the cart, jumped into the stream and attached the ropes firmly around the drowning pony's body. They tied them to the cart and with all of them pulling and straining, they managed to haul the limp and cold pony onto the bank. There he lay quite lifeless even though they dried him off, rubbed his ears and put old corn sacks over him to warm his blood.

After an hour of trying to revive the pony, Jed decided to give up, despite Sinni and Manfri begging him to try something, anything to bring him back to life. "We's done our best," was all he would say. Reluctantly they loaded up the cart, he told his cob to walk on and they headed for home. After about a mile, the despondent silence of the children turned into disbelieving whoops of joy as they first heard and then saw the shape of a little roan pony getting closer and closer as he trotted to catch them up. The half-drowned pony had got his strength back after a rest, scrambled to his feet and then proceeded to follow them all the way home. He took some nursing to get him back to health as he had huge bite wounds in his neck where the stallion had attacked him.

Romany Gypsies possess an uncanny gift of curing horses with potions made from honey, herbs and hedgerow plants. Manfri kept that information to himself, but continued to finish the tale to his now captivated audience. He described how Uncle Jed and his friends were sitting around a fire that evening talking about the strange events of the day. Jed told them he had been convinced the pony was 'brown bread'. That is a slang term, it's Cockney Rhyming slang for 'dead'. On hearing this, Sinni had piped up with "Do you mean brown bread like Hovis, Uncle?" Jed had roared with laughter and answered, "Well that's him named then! We'll call him Hovis."

After such a splendid and exciting story, Fred and Cindy were stars of the show. The children had loved how the pony had got his name at the end. Fred added more drama and detail by saying "… an' you should'a seen the holes in his neck, big as me fist they was! But we mended him up a treat, hardly a mark there now!"

I grew to love those two, they knew who I was right from the start. Well, gypsies have an affinity with horses and as soon as they saw me, Manfri had whispered to his sister in a broken Romany tongue, "Miri pen, dik acai the rinkeno koshto grai! Dik at his yoks, he's tatcho, he's got ozi!" Loosely translated, he'd said, "My sister, look at the beautiful wooden horse! Look at his eyes, he's real, he's got heart and soul!" They often referred to me as their little 'Koshengro' which literally means 'Wood fellow'. I just loved this simple yet poetic term for me. I don't think they'd ever seen a rocking horse before.

The pair told me many secrets during our stay at the Rectory. Their biggest secret was how they had hidden Hovis away to keep him safe during the war. Their uncle had been called up to fight and the Government was taking so many horses, they decided to hide Hovis somewhere he could wait for them until the war was over. I always keep secrets, so I can't tell you where they hid him, but I CAN tell you it was a brilliantly clever plan!

My time at the Orphanage was drawing to a close. I'd spent four hard but happy and fulfilling years with all those lovely children whom I hope went on to make a success of their lives. On the other hand, the end of the war spelled uncertainty and disappointment for me, and later, a tragedy nearly ended my life. Perhaps I HAD started to make my own luck though, for my meeting with the gypsy family was the saving of me.

CHAPTER 5
'OLD LONELY'

1919

The war had officially ended a year earlier, much to the heartfelt relief of everybody. But the damage done and horror of what had taken place shocked every man, woman and child alive. The country was in tatters, people were grieving for the dead and jobs and wages were hard to come by. The Orphanage was closed down, some of the children moved into other institutions or foster homes, but others were old enough to leave in search of apprenticeships. I was delighted when my lovely gypsy children were reunited with their uncle. He had been wounded, but returned to where he knew the children had been left. It was a joyous day when he arrived in his flat cart to take them home. What a sad farewell we had. Before they left, they did a strange thing.

Not many knew about my hidden pommel hole, but like me, secrets were their speciality so of course they knew! There is no official word in their language for 'secret', they would just whisper "Tel te jib!" (Hold your tongue!) or "Rokka nanti" (Say nothing). Sinni fetched a twig from the garden and solemnly bent it in half. She passed it to Manfri who carefully posted it though the hole under my saddle flap where it quietly dropped into my belly. I was mystified, but they read my thoughts and explained that the stick was part of a secret gypsy trail called the 'patrin'. Sticks, stones, strewn leaves or tufts of grass would be placed on the ground in a special way to signify which direction a band of gypsies had travelled. This allowed families to keep in contact. This strange secret was their gift to me. Manfri's parting words were a sort of promise. "Now you have that kosht (wood) in yer belly, we'll meet up again. We'll find ya wherever ya be… an' kushti bok (good luck) to ya!"

"One may have a blazing hearth in one's soul, and yet no one ever comes to sit by it."
— **Vincent Van Gogh.**

To be honest, I almost forgot about the twig incident. I was too excited thinking of another promise made to me at the start of the war. Annie had said the family would all come back when it was over. The Rectory was now empty. Everyone had left, the Warden was needed elsewhere and Matron had volunteered at another refuge for injured soldiers who had returned with a condition called 'shell-shock'. Before they went, they tidied up the house as best they could and I heard them talking about the Rector returning to his old parish. Before they slammed the door shut for the last time, Matron glanced back at me and said, "Well done, Sonny, you did a good job with those little 'uns! Your lot will be back with you soon!"

All that was left were some broken beds, piles of damp drapes and torn blankets, the old tin bath and a box of grubby toys that had been donated to the children. And ME, of course. But I wasn't worried. I was fully expecting my lovely Tubb family to return any day and life to go on at the Rectory as it had before the awful nightmare of the last few years. I was hoping we could get back to normal as if nothing had ever happened. So I waited patiently, all alone in the old cold empty Rectory. I waited and I waited. I was so sure they would come through the front door with all their warmth, smiles and laughter. I imagined their delight at seeing me, still alive and well, the house being returned to a home full of chatter, cooking aromas and the wonderful music I longed to hear.

Loneliness is one of the saddest of conditions. Like a real horse, I needed the company of others. But as a rocking horse, I'd grown to love people, especially children and it was my job and pleasure to keep them happily amused. I admit I needed to feel wanted and loved, so being totally alone was pure torture for me. I began to realise the awful truth. No one was coming. It was at times like this that I again wondered if I'd have preferred not to have a heart…

How long did I wait? It felt like years but in truth it was probably several months. I'd never felt so sad and abandoned. I think I know why the Tubbs never returned. Sometime after the Warden locked up and left, three women came to the front door and knocked loudly. My heart jumped and raced. Had someone come for me? I'd swung myself to a position between the front door and window, so I could see and hear anything that happened in the street. It helped to relieve my awful feeling of isolation. Now it allowed me to see that the women were holding a large black wreath made of leaves and twigs (which reminded me briefly about the twig that Manfri had dropped in my belly) which were cleverly twisted together. Two names were written on a card attached to it, but I couldn't make them out. As they sombrely hung the wreath on the front door, I heard them say how dreadfully sad that the Rector had lost his two sons in the war. One killed in action and the other missing, presumed dead. They also said the Tubbs obviously hadn't come back but they couldn't blame them for not wanting to return to their old family home. The memories would be too painful to bear.

Well, that news made me feel even more wretched. Oh, poor Tom and young Bertie! How absolutely terrible. Mrs Tubb was so proud of her sons, I couldn't imagine her grief. Annie and her sisters must be suffering too, losing their darling brothers. It was all too grim. I understood that it also meant I was abandoned for good. No matter that I was nearly twenty years old, a bit scruffy and well-used with less hair than I once had, what mattered now was that I was ownerless, unloved and unwanted.

Then life took a turn for the worse. Although I'd been on my own for months staying in that damp house, at least I was sheltered from the icy rain and wind of the fast approaching winter. One awful day, some rough workmen kicked the Rectory door open, talking in loud voices about the work that lay ahead for them. Apparently, they had been instructed to 'gut the whole place' ready for renovation and building work. "Rip everything out and we'll make a massive bonfire out the back to get rid of it all, save carting it all away." My heart lurched at the word 'bonfire'. Being made of wood, I was aware how dangerous any form of fire could be to us rocking horses. It was the one thing that could kill us very quickly. Whenever a log fire had been blazing in the parlour hearth, Mrs Tubb had always warned the children to move me away in case I was singed by a flying ember or my tail was set alight.

The workmen hardly noticed me but when they did, one said, "Ha, look at Old Lonely No Mates over there! Poor ole nag's seen better days!" They made use of me as a clothes horse, piling all the dirty curtains and bedding on my back and neck. They would come in and hang their coats and caps on my ears and say jokingly, "Lonely looks good in that hat!" If anything went missing, they'd shout out, "Have a look on Old Lonely, that's where most things end up!" The house was freezing; I'd never felt so cold. Rain dripped in through the missing slates on the roof. I became filthy with dirt, plaster dust and grime as they proceeded to strip wallpaper, pull down beams and ceilings. After a couple of weeks, the rooms were bare and the house was a shell. Then I heard those dreaded words: "What'll we do with the toy hoss?" "Drag the old nag out the back and chuck it on the pile ready for the bonfire tomorrow. It should go up a treat with that lump of wood on top!" And drag me they certainly did. They knocked me over and with ropes around my swing stand I was unceremoniously hauled out through those beautiful French windows and down the garden path to my certain death. Although those old rags they had thrown on my body managed to protect me a little bit, the pain of being dragged along the ground was unbearable. My legs creaked; my already straggly mane and tail were ripped out on passing briars. Even more lamentable, my beautiful dappled paintwork, painstakingly given to me by Florence, was being scraped and scuffed. Then two hefty men flung me onto the heap of rotten timbers and house debris. "We'll come back tomorrow, lads, and set it alight!" were the last dreadful words I heard as night fell in the Rectory garden. I knew my end was near.

Then a strange thing happened. As I lay helpless on that huge pile of rubbish, memories of my life flashed before me. I saw my kindly Maker's face at the workshop, darling sweet Gracie and my old friend Cobweb in the attic. I felt Annie's hands on my neck and saw all the little orphans that had played on me. But then, a clear picture of the dark-haired brother and sister, Manfri and Sinni, stayed in my head and would not leave me. As I'd been dragged to the unlit bonfire, I'd felt all the bits that were in my belly rattling about — a piece of my ear, a wooden knob, several boiled sweets and the bent twig. But the twig seemed the most important. You have to make your own luck in life – so I decided to try something to save myself. I tried to reach the gypsy children with my thoughts. All night I tried to alert them to my fate and ask them for help, all within my head. Hadn't they said that once they'd given me that twig, they'd find me wherever I was and that we'd meet up again? Manfri had wished me good luck. Well, I was calling in that luck now…

CHAPTER 6
'BOKTALO GRAI'

1920

Thank goodness... I'm still here, alive and well! I can't quite believe the strange and wonderful way that I was saved. I still marvel at it. Nowadays, I live with two real ponies and the gypsy family who rescued me. Oh, and a thieving lurcher dog called Fly. Uncle Jed officially adopted his brother's children to ensure they could not be taken from him to end up in an institution for waifs. Our home is a rambling, run-down but pleasant old house and yard in Oil Drum Alley. We are in a poor area of Hammersmith called Shepherd's Bush, well-known for its close-knit community of totters and scrap metal dealers. The house sits in a cobbled street about five miles from my old home, the Rectory. Jed had taught his wards to be successful totters and he was always giving them wise tips. He told them that although the Rectory's area of London was a twenty-minute trot away, it was worth the journey as there were rich pickings to be had, because a better class of folk live there. "Their tat is us's treasure!" he would declare, with a crafty twinkle in his eye.

Now I will tell you about the day I was rescued from certain death. Adults would explain what happened as a pure 'coincidence'. Perhaps I've spent too much time with children; they don't believe in coincidence, they believe in magic and I think I agree with them, for what happened that day was driven by magic. It was the morning of November 5th, which is Guy Fawkes Day. The day commemorates this villain's failure to blow up the Houses of Parliament with his 'Gunpowder Plot'. Huge bonfires are lit in the evening and the highlight of the celebration is the ritual burning of the 'Guy'. This is an effigy of Fawkes; often a figure made of straw and dressed in old clothes, like a doll. It's a horrid tradition as people would place the Guy on the fire and watch it burn. As I lay in the Rectory garden trapped high up on that rubbish heap, I very much feared that I would be the Guy when the workmen returned to set their bonfire alight.

The early morning of November 5th was cold and frosty. I felt chilled to the grain of my wood from being out all night on that bonfire pile and I was completely drained from my frantic night's thoughts. I had no idea if these pleas for help had managed to reach my gypsy children. As I gazed around sadly at the overgrown garden that I thought would be my last resting place, my ears suddenly picked up on familiar sounds coming ever nearer. The thud of a solitary pony's hooves, the creak and rumble of small cartwheels, the jingle of harness being undone and strains of conversation in that strange Romany language, spoken in hushed whispers. Then, pushing their way through the bushes appeared two ragged figures, a man and woman carrying a bundle and leading a small roan-coloured pony. They stopped short of the bonfire heap and set him free to graze the lush grass that had sprung up all around. After collecting some dry twigs and dead branches, they proceeded to light a small sheltered fire surrounded by stones. I wasn't at all afraid; it was as controlled and comforting as a parlour fire. A tiny bit of heat actually reached my frozen body and felt so good. The roan pony grazed closer and closer to me, circling the heap where I lay stranded on my side above him.

It's strange, but even though I was feeling so awful, as I looked down on the little pony, I couldn't help but admire his beautiful eye-catching colour. I'd never seen anything like it! He was like a little dark brown Christmas pudding that had been doused in icing sugar or a shiny conker that had been frosted over during a cold night. His rich brown head sported a white star between his eyes and his body was of the same colour but completely overlaid with a frosting of white hairs. In contrast, his mane and tail were an admixture of white, grey, black and silver hairs that added to his unusual beauty. Although I also saw an ugly jagged scar on his neck, in my state of exhaustion I still didn't realise the identity of this little horse. I expect you've guessed, though.

The couple were an older man and woman, squatting huddled over their fire trying to warm themselves. They were hungrily eating food they'd taken from their bundle whilst deep in conversation. By now I was consumed with curiosity and strained to hear their conversation spoken in pure Romany. This was hard to understand but I got the gist of what they were saying—and everything was beginning to make sense. It was as if all the pieces of a jigsaw puzzle were fitting together. They were discussing their long, exhausting journey all the way up from the New Forest to London with pony and cart. It had taken them over three weeks, but they congratulated themselves on finding the Rectory. Jed had told them the place had been a sanctuary for the children during those awful war years. From what I could understand, it appeared the woman was Jed's sister and she and her husband had been asked to keep an eye on the children's much loved pony during the war. Yes, the roan pony was little Hovis in Manfri's story! This was the big secret that they'd told me about, how they had hidden him to stop him from being taken to war.

The family had turned him loose to run free with all the wild ponies that lived in the New Forest. The forester farmers who owned the ponies had gathered theirs up every autumn, but as Hovis didn't have their brand on him, he was left behind each winter to fend for himself. This is how he managed to escape being sold into the Army during those war years. The Lovells, as the couple were called, had caught him up when the danger had passed and kept him safe with them. When the time was right, they'd decided to make the long journey to London to meet Jed and the children and return Hovis safely. Now, they said, it was up to the family to find the secret trail of leaves, grasses and twigs bent like arrows that they had carefully laid all around the area of the Rectory. They hoped the trails would lead them to this very garden. "All we has to do now is wait... an' hope." They finished the sentence in English, as if for my benefit. Well, I knew all about waiting! But I, of course, didn't have very long; the workmen would be coming back to set me alight and if they saw the Lovells, the police would surely be called. Even if the family managed to meet up, would any of them find me lying on that heap, or would I be left to die?

Manfri and Sinni had set off that same morning with their new chestnut mare pulling the London trolley. They left Oil Drum Alley and headed to the 'better off' end of town hoping to pick up some quality 'tat' and make their uncle proud. After trotting four miles at a spanking pace, they gave the mare a breather and let her walk to catch her breath. Suddenly Sinni shouted to her brother, "Oiy oiy, Manfri, pull up, I thinks I saw us a patrin (gypsy trail) on the side there!" Excitedly, they followed the signs which they recognised as their family's own. It took them along the route straight towards the area of the Rectory, but after a mile the grasses were strewn around haphazardly and the twigs had been kicked about by passers-by. They'd lost the trail. Being so near to their old home, the children decided to go to there anyway as they'd heard it was empty and the thought of finding some scrap iron there pleased them.

We heard them arrive around midday. The Lovells jumped up and the children ran to greet them. What a happy reunion I witnessed. There were lots of hugs and whoops of joy with them dancing around the dying embers of the fire. Sinni had rushed up to Hovis, flung her arms around his neck and buried her face in his mane. Of course, even after four years, he recognised his rescuers and seemed happy with all the attention. They sat and talked for a while and although I was so pleased for them, I began to worry they would never see me. I used the thoughts in my head again, trying to get someone to look in my direction. It worked. Manfri gazed at the pile of rubbish and scanned for anything that could be taken home as scrap. He spotted the old tin bath, laughing at the memories of those parlour bath nights; he told his sister to climb up to retrieve it. Sinni scrambled up, treading nearer and nearer to my head. Then she exclaimed excitedly to the others, "Oooh, I thinks I's found a groini (gemstone), a sparklin' groini an' it's big as a lump o vonga (coal) but brown an' shining!" Carefully she scraped away the rags and matted hair on my face to properly reveal my eye, my glass eye glistening with joy at seeing her lovely face. Sinni gasped in wonder and whispered unbelievingly, "Sonny?"

She screamed down to her brother that she'd found their koshengro, the little wooden horse with a heart and it wasn't a jewel she'd seen but his big brown eye! She began clearing all the filthy rubbish off my body. Everybody joined in to free me and when they found the ropes around my damaged stand, they carefully pulled on these till I slid down to land on the soft grass. I couldn't help thinking it reminded me of Hovis' story, when they'd pulled him out of the water to rescue him. Now they were rescuing me too. With a few tugs and kicks, they freed me from my badly broken swing stand and stood me up on just my bare hooves. It felt lovely to be upright, no longer trapped waiting to be burned alive. I'm sure I looked a bedraggled mess, but the Lovells were impressed by my obvious good breeding. They, of course, knew a fine horse when they saw one. Mr Lovell declared, "That's one boktalo grai (lucky horse) if ever there were!" They all realised the fate that had been awaiting me: I would have gone up in flames.

After having gathered as much scrap as they could find, they placed me carefully on the trolley, resting me on old tarpaulins so I wouldn't suffer any more damage. With everyone loaded and ready, the children drove the chestnut mare home followed closely by Hovis and the Lovells.

An hour later, the workmen arrived to have their bonfire. They were mystified because I was missing from the heap. "Old Lonely

No Mates is gorn off the top," one shouted. Another spotted my splintered stand and the tatty ropes lying in the garden and saw Hovis' hoof prints in the ground nearby. "Blimey O'Riley!" he said, "Reckon the bloomin' fairies have nicked Old Lonely an' ridden off with him!" The first man answered, "Good job an' all. Didn't seem right t' burn the liddle toy hoss..."

CHAPTER 7
'BOKKY'

1920 was a simply lovely year for me and I settled into life with my gypsy family as if I'd been born to it. They were kind, fair and gentle folk. I seemed to have friends all around me, which helped me to recover from my near-death experience. Yes, I was badly frightened by what had happened but now life seemed even sweeter for it! When we all returned from the Rectory that November afternoon, there was a great celebration. Their Uncle Jed had to calm the children down to make any sense of the tale that tumbled from their mouths. He was overjoyed to see his dear relatives and so grateful to them for fulfilling their promise and bringing the little roan pony home safely. He was also surprised to see a small carved horse on the cart. Of course, Jed had heard all about ME from Sinni. I had been her friend in the orphanage; the wooden horse with the pretty little head, big brown eyes that could see, and a heart that could keep secrets deep in his soul. Jed never doubted that I had life in me. He congratulated the youngsters on how clever they had been to see the family trail, to have found the Lovells and for my rescue.

On our return, I was stabled in one of the three stalls in the yard on a deep bed of straw, just like the other two real ponies. We all got a rub down; well, I got a careful wash with a sponge and soapy water to remove all the grime that was plastered on me. The Lovells warned Jed not to put Hovis next to the mare as he was still nervous of other horses since being savagely attacked all those years ago. He didn't trust many horses or people. "Best put the liddle spotted hoss in the middle of 'em. Bokky won't do him no harm." I loved my new name. 'Bokky' (short for boktalo) means 'lucky' and every time I heard it, I remembered just how true it was. So, I stood on my own four feet just like a proper horse, between the two, and developed a real friendship with them. We talked whenever we could, in between their work shifts doing the totting rounds. Hovis was shy and quiet but very clever at knowing how to survive because, after all, he was half wild. The chestnut mare was loud, flashy and could be moody, but she told us some good stories that kept us amused. The lurcher dog Fly lived with us too. He was often curled up fast asleep in our straw beds or mooching around looking for food—but he was as quick as lightning when it came to despatching any rodents that dared come into our stable looking for oats.

"There is no more precious gift that that of knowledge." – **Attributed to Plato**

Manfri and Sinni were now 13 and 11 years old respectively. The Council knew they lived with their uncle but were concerned that the children had never attended school. They deemed it necessary that the pair should be given some education so they could at least be able to read and write. So Manfri and his sister were sent to the local school. The children of gypsies, more commonly known as travellers nowadays, often had a bad time in education. When the other children found out that they came from a different background, they would be teased, bullied and even attacked in the playground. Manfri was always in trouble for fighting with boys who taunted Sinni and many received a bloodied nose because of it! They both felt thoroughly miserable. Luckily, a lovely teacher who had taken an interest in the pair saw how unhappy they were and decided to talk to the headmaster. She told him the problem and asked if she could visit them at home to give them their lessons. She also promised that she would set them tests every now and then to show the school how they were progressing. The headmaster agreed willingly as he didn't like the disruptions their presence was causing. Their uncle agreed to this plan and the children were delighted. They had really taken to this wonderful lady who always seemed to be on their side. She was more than just their teacher; she was becoming a dear friend. So, this was how the school mistress, Mrs Grace Smyth came into our lives, or should I say came BACK into my life…

I heard her before I saw her. I instantly recognised her voice as she entered the family's yard and greeted the children. Yes, it was the unmistakably sweet voice of Gracie from Kilwick Manor; no longer mousy and in the shadow of her mean brother, but a lovely grown-up Gracie, still as gentle and caring as I remembered her. She was now a beautiful young woman, a teacher who also did charity work helping families who were struggling after the war. My heart was racing as I glimpsed her through the grubby stable window, going into the house with the children to start their lessons. She had no idea I was standing in the stalls with the ponies. I was aching to meet her, to see if she'd know who I was after all these years. About an hour later, they came out of the house and headed towards us in the yard. I needn't have worried, I should have known the children would want to show her Hovis and tell her all about his rescue, and maybe even about how they'd saved me from the bonfire. Sinni was dragging her teacher by her hand, nearer and nearer until I could see her clearly because of the natural turn of my head.

As Grace entered the stable and saw me, she gasped in surprise. "Sinni, you've got a rocking horse? You didn't say! I thought you meant a real horse...where's his stand? Oh, I l LOVE rocking horses, I used to have one..." Then she looked harder at me, saw my old torn ear and gasped again and with her hand to her mouth, whispered, "Oh Goodness, it's Blizzie...it really is Blizzie! I can't believe it's darling little Blizzie!" Sinni was a bit put out, and replied solemnly, "Ee IS a real hoss, Miss." Then Grace explained the whole story of how she knew me, that I was actually her brother's rocking horse and that hers was called Cobweb and we had lived in the attic of Kilwick Manor. Manfri asked if hers had been a dapple grey like me and exclaimed he thought it a wonderful name. She told them how I'd gone to live at the Rectory with her school friends when her brother was given his own pony. With tears in her eyes, she told us how distraught she'd been when Cobweb had been taken away by the grooms at the start of the war. She had no idea where he was now. My heart sank at this news. I just hoped he'd survived the war and had been as lucky as I had.

Manfri finished the last piece of the jigsaw tale, telling Grace how they'd met me when I'd been left behind in the Rectory, which then became a refuge for orphans. They also told her about gifting me with the twig, which ultimately brought them back to me when I was in mortal danger. She'd looked confused until they explained about the secret gypsy 'patrin' trail. Then the three of them held each other's hands to encircle me and next leaned in to give me a huge hug. Grace said, "It's like a fairy tale…and of COURSE I know he's real!"

All that summer Grace Smyth visited daily to teach the children. Because they had formed such a close friendship with their teacher, the two absorbed their lessons well and managed to pass the little tests that were set for them, proving they could read and write to a reasonable standard. Often, Grace used our stable as a classroom; the children seemed to concentrate better with us and Fly listening on and lending our quiet support. Grace found Manfri and Sinni to be extremely bright, both possessing wonderful retentive memories. She marvelled at their account of their previous life down in the New Forest. To give them confidence, she told them how clever they really were. They explained how Jed had taught them to use a knife and carve and shave hazel or elder sticks to make curly chrysanthemums. These wooden flowers were called 'roozlums'; the children would dye them with blackberry or beetroot juice and then would go door to door selling them for a few pennies. She said not many children had the skill to fashion things like that or could read secret chalk marks left on walls or follow trails. She didn't know of any who could take their dog out to catch a rabbit and cook it for their tea! How clever they were to be able to make a fire and a shelter out of willow rods and sacks. She remarked that they were far better than her at knowing what could be eaten safely when foraging for food, or what herbs to pick to make medicines. All these compliments made them feel proud to be gypsies. Their sort of education, she said, was different but just as valuable as school lessons and now they knew both! Grace just knew how to make people feel good about themselves and I loved her for it. There was always a loving stroke or hug for me whenever Grace was in the stable, but I noticed a wistful look in her eyes. I think she really missed Cobweb…

Uncle Jed taught them how to shave hazel sticks into curly flowers.

One day, when autumn was approaching, with the wind rattling the trees and rain beating on the stable roof, Grace told the children that I, as a rocking horse, would suffer damage if I was left out all winter. My wood may swell or warp if I got damp and my gesso could crack. They looked very worried and asked what should be done. Grace had married an antique dealer called Archie Smyth who had fought in the war and on his safe return, had started up his own business in a small shop. They lived above the shop which was in the better end of town. Grace said Archie knew all about rocking horses and often mended them so that they could still be ridden by their owners. She would ask him the best course of action.

Our life continued in this happy vein right up until Christmas. Oh, I do remember that on the evening of November 5th – which marked a whole year had passed since my bonfire experience – sweet Sinni came to me and gently wrapped my head in an old curtain. She whispered that it was to make sure I didn't see or hear any of the terrifying bangs and flashes of fireworks. She wanted to protect me from bad memories and didn't want me to be scared. I was so touched by her empathy that I put up with the stuffy curtain – it actually reminded me of that day twenty years ago when I first arrived at Kilwick Manor, my head draped in those thick grey blankets…

Also in November, Archie Smyth had visited the yard to inspect me at Gracie's request. I suppose I haven't spoken much about how I looked now. This is not because I am embarrassed at what I'd become, but more that I had changed and didn't think it mattered so much. To be honest, I'm surprised Gracie even recognised me! Much of my beautiful dappled paintwork was scratched and faded, my once luxurious mane and tail were thinned to a straggle and my tack and saddle cloth were worn and threadbare, my rosettes were long gone… But my heart, soul and spirits were fine and that's what matters in life.

Archie looked me over carefully and then turned to the others to say that I was a very well-made English Dapple Grey, from the Leach firm he guessed, and I showed all the hallmarks of having had a skilled maker. He insisted I should be put back on a stand for my own safety, because if I fell, I may break a limb or even my neck. He added that perhaps a new mane and tail would be beneficial and maybe a bit of work on my body to protect my original paintwork. He told the family that although I was only twenty years old now, in the future I would become a valuable antique worth many hundreds of pounds. Apparently, Archie had found and saved a horse dating from 1820 and after restoring it, sold it for a lot of money, which had helped him buy his own shop. I felt so proud that day, but the pride I felt was different: it was because I was a good rocking horse and that my maker's quality work had been recognised by an expert.

On hearing Archie's verdict, Sinni went into Hovis' stall and told him that I needed some hair in my poor mane and tail. She asked him if she could take some of his, as he had SUCH a thick abundance of hair and he really wouldn't miss it. Grace had explained to us that buying a horse-hair set to replace mine would be rather expensive. So, the idea was to take some of Hovis' hair and cleverly weave and plait it through my existing mane. My tail would be a lot easier to add to. I loved this plan as I felt it would be an honour to wear a bit of my dear friend Hovis close to me (and I'd always marvelled at the colours in his tail!). He agreed, and when Sinni had cut off plenty of long strands, they went ahead with the skilled work; Sinni using her knowledge of basket making and Grace, her expertise in plaiting up the horses she had ridden in shows. Archie came back to the yard one weekend with his tools and a beautiful second-hand stand. Once I'd been re-attached, standing tall and strong again, he worked on my body to make me almost as good as new! It was such a kind gesture, an early Christmas present for the children. From then on, the children made sure I wore a thick jute rug, just like the other two. This was placed on me every night to keep the damp off my repaired dapples.

My time at my home in Oil Drum Alley was drawing to a close. It was now nearing the end of December and the children invited the Smyths to spend Christmas day with them. After sharing a huge feast with the family indoors, they all came out to the yard near our stable, where the fire-pit was lit and everyone sat around on upturned buckets. Their old, blackened kettle was set to boil for making tea, hanging above the fire on its iron rod and hook. The children roasted chestnuts and marshmallows in the flames and happily joined in to relate stories that were told by each person in turn. I had been carefully brought out into the yard as a treat for young Sinni. Now I was back on my new swing stand, she loved to sit on me and have a quiet rock when there was any sort of social gathering. It felt wonderful being ridden again and in the centre of that lovely happy clan. I listened contentedly to all the chatter but what I heard said at the end of the afternoon gave me a shock. It seemed the family had decided to move on. Jed announced it was time to leave London as they had made their 'bit o' money', enough to allow them to travel again. "Us gypsies are travellers. T'is wot us lot do best, we's have to move on, ne'er in one place too long. That's our way, the true Romany way." As evening drew in, daylight faded, the fire died down and everyone fell silent at the thought of the big change to come. Once again, I felt fear in the pit of my stomach, fear of an uncertain future, just when I'd found peace and contentment.

Is it possible to be very sad yet very happy, all at the same time? I didn't think I could ever feel that way, but that's exactly how I felt about what happened next in my strange but colourful life.

Chapter 8 'Lucky'

"Happiness is a butterfly which when pursued, is always just beyond your grasp but which, if you will sit down quietly, may alight upon you."
– **Nathaniel Hawthorne.**

1921 was the start of a long and wonderful period in my life when I truly felt that happiness, like a butterfly, had alighted on me. At first, when I heard the family was moving away, I was filled with doubts and sadness. Would I be taken or left behind? Was I to lose the very dear friends I had made? I loved both the gypsies and their ponies, but couldn't bear the thought of losing Grace all over again. She made me feel good and I loved being near her; she was that sort of person. If I was left in the yard, what would become of me? Oh, how I would miss the children! Soon, my future became clear. Plans were being discussed and I managed to overhear conversations in Romany which were within earshot of my stall. The family planned to move on soon after Christmas, before the weather took a turn for the worse, as it often did during February and March. They aimed to over-winter down in the New Forest until spring, when they would travel about to horse fairs and find work fruit picking during the summer months. I also heard them mention that they hoped to visit the famous Epsom Derby in June to meet up with the rest of their clan. And to the question of what would happen to me? No, I would not be going with them. I should have realised that I was far too heavy and awkward to go that far on a trolley cart and there was certainly no room for me in their living wagons.

It had been decided by Jed's family that I should be given to their much-loved friend Grace Smyth as a farewell present. They said for the good of my health, they knew I should be living indoors like a "posh toy hoss oughta". I thought it so kind of them to consider my well-being and wonderful for me to be going to live with the Smyths. But I knew I would miss Manfri and Sinni dreadfully, I would miss the friendship of the dog and ponies and the outdoor life I'd grown to love. That's the trouble with possessing a heart. At times, your emotions can tear you apart.

True to their word, in January the gypsy family headed off with their wagons and carts on the long journey down to the Forest. I went to live in the pretty little flat above the antique shop with Grace and her husband. Before we parted, Manfri whispered in my ear, "We ain't sayin' G'bye, Bokky, we's sayin' use yer sherro (head) like ya did afore, if ya ever needs us…" Then he slipped a miniature wooden 'roozlum', a tiny carved flower-head, through my pommel hole down into my belly as a token of luck. Would I ever see them again? Well, you never knew with travellers…

Grace and Archie had made a warm and inviting home for themselves. Compared to Kilwick, this cosy flat comprising three small rooms and a kitchen must have seemed quite tiny. I could tell Grace was glowingly content here and they clearly loved each other very much. She was so delighted when I was gifted to her; even Archie had looked pleased as he'd carefully carried me up their narrow stairs. I stood in pride of place in their sitting room by the prettily curtained back window and far enough away from the coal fire to be safe. To my utter joy, Archie was in the habit of playing soothing classical music on a very modern looking gramophone. He would come up from a busy day in the shop and as Grace prepared them a supper, he would flop down in the beautiful antique leather armchair by the fire and listen happily to his music. He told Grace it relaxed him and washed all the cares of the day away. I was in my element and understood perfectly. It had been so long since I had heard that calming yet stirring sound I loved. I soon became familiar with many composers and learned their music off by heart. I still loved Bach best but now I appreciated Scarlatti, Satie and others. If I DID start to sway again without being aware of it, Archie never noticed as his eyes were always shut as if he were asleep. I don't think he ever realised that I had a heart and was what I am; certainly Gracie never shared our secret with him.

About a year later, something happened that changed our fortunes for ever. During the war, Kilwick Manor had been given over to the Royal Army Medical Corps to be used as a hospital for wounded soldiers. When Grace left to marry Archie, her father had told her to take some of the furniture for their new home and any of the family paintings and ornaments that she wanted. Her father now worked for the Government and Gus had been found a job acquiring horses for the army. Apparently, a close doctor friend of his father's had declared that Gus had not been medically fit enough to fight as a soldier. After the war, Kilwick had been sold off and they had moved far away to another county. Grace had lost touch with her family, but she really didn't seem to mind.

Most of the smaller pieces of the Manor's furniture had managed to fit into their flat but the other items were stored in Archie's shed at the rear of the shop. One day when business was rather slow, he decided to sort out a few articles that were of no sentimental value to Grace which might be sold in the shop. I watched from my top window as he pulled everything out, made a pile in the courtyard and then called his wife to decide what to do with it all. She rummaged about excitedly, saying that she'd not seen some things for years and how she loved this or didn't much care for that. But then her mood changed and her expression darkened when she saw the last item right at the bottom of Archie's heap. This was an old painting in a very ornate frame. It was beautifully done in oils and was even signed by a famous artist, but it was of a grim subject and depicted an unfortunate horse being attacked by a ferocious beast that was clawing at its back. Grace told her husband that she had always hated that painting as it used to give her nightmares when she was a child. She begged him to sell it immediately; she didn't even want it hanging up in the shop where she may catch a glimpse of it.

Poor Grace was quite upset and came rushing upstairs to sit by me. This was her usual habit when Archie was working, but now she was distraught and I couldn't understand why. Grace always called me Lucky these days, never Blizzie or even Bokki. She told me how she'd been sorting through everything and then discovered the offending Kilwick painting. "I don't even know how we ever came to have that awful picture." She frowned and thought for a minute, adding in an angry tone, "Do you know something, Lucky? I bet you Gus sneaked it in with the rest of the pile I was taking. He knew full well that it would upset me dreadfully!" I can't say I was surprised…

Isn't life funny sometimes? Gus's nasty trick backfired badly on him and turned out very nicely for us. I won't go into detail, but the painting was worth an absolute fortune! Archie didn't hang it in the shop as Grace had asked, but took it to be valued by a large gallery who wanted to buy it and immediately offered a huge sum for it. The Smyths were delighted and couldn't believe their good luck. Very soon after, the couple decided to move house. There was such excitement in the flat as Archie and Grace discussed where they would go and what sort of house they would like. Nothing too big like the cold Manor House, but with more space than their flat offered. They agreed they'd love something really pretty and old, with a history. Then Grace dropped a very large hint to Archie: she said she'd really like a house that had room for a nursery.

Of course, I already knew Grace's secret. She was going to have a baby. During one of our talks together, Grace had told me how much she loved her job teaching her children and how much she wished for a child of her own one day. She said, "I know that's the one thing missing in your life too, Lucky. You love them as much as I do. We both need children, that would make our lives perfect…" Not long after, she'd confided in me by whispering in my ear that soon I'd have a little one to rock to sleep and she was going to buy a baby-basket to strap to my saddle. I couldn't have been happier.

When Archie finally understood that he was going to be a father, he was overjoyed. He said the move would come just in time to welcome a new life into our family. In the fullness of time, the perfect property was found and bought with the fortune from that painting. So we moved to a county close to London but with so many trees and rolling downs, it felt like we were a lot further away. Through the top vent window of the removal van that transported me and our belongings, I managed to see most of the journey and our eventual destination.

Our new home was quite beautiful and I'll do my best to describe it. This was the prettiest thatched red brick cottage that I'd ever seen. It stood within its grounds of lawn, a well-stocked garden and an oak-framed barn. There were cherry and lilac trees everywhere and an ancient, twisted wisteria framing the front door. Known as Brambler Cottage, it was situated down a tiny lane in the small hamlet of Hidley, not many miles from the famous racecourse on Epsom Downs. It was large and airy for such an old place, with plenty of room to raise a family. Archie hoped his business would flourish in this well-chosen location as it wasn't too far for him to travel back to the auction houses of London, where he bought and sold antiques. The barn would be converted into a workshop and store. Grace was delighted with their new abode. "Where shall we put Lucky?" she asked Archie. "He can reside in our very best room. That little horse is our lucky charm, for sure!"

1923 was the year we had moved house. In October of that year, the Smyths welcomed their adored baby girl into our little family. We were complete and totally content. A basket seat was fitted to my saddle and I was responsible for either lulling little Isabel to sleep or giving her a thrilling ride, rocking her safely in her wicker seat.

1932. My life could not have been more perfect, watching young Izzy (everyone called her that) grow into a delightful child under the guidance of her sweet and loving parents. She adored horses and, luckily for her, there were many around our area. Every day she would spot a string of prancing racehorses going past the window or when she was taken to her school near Epsom, she'd see them galloping on the downs.

I like to think it was my early influence that had fuelled her passion for horses. Izzy, like her mother, often came to me to talk about what had happened during her day. She would return from school and run to me to describe the various trainers' horses she had recognised whilst out exercising. "None of them are quite as wonderful as you, Lucky, but there's one I see every day on the downs and he might run in the Derby!" Izzy was well and truly bitten by the racing bug and although only nine years old, she already had a desire to spend her life with horses. Ethel Yates was her best friend at school. Ethel's father, Bert, worked for a racehorse trainer and she had her own pony which was stabled at the yard in Epsom. Izzy and Ethel would groom and ride the pony every weekend. It was noticed that Grace's daughter was a natural rider and her mother would remark it was because she had been taught so well by me. I was still good at my job and it made me proud.

"Hope springs eternal in the human breast..."
– **Alexander Pope.**

For the next few weeks leading up to the world-famous race, the Epsom Derby, there was a buzz of excitement in the air. One of Epsom's own horses, trained in the town, was entered to run in the big race. No one seriously thought he could win; after all, it had been nearly one hundred years since an Epsom-trained horse had managed that feat! Despite only a small possibility of him winning, everyone who lived in or near the town was gripped with race-day fever and decided to bet on this local horse to show their support. The colt was a handsome bay fellow called April the Fifth and his trainer was a very popular local character. Not only did this man ride as a jockey and train horses by day, he was also an entertainer, comedian and actor, who owned his own theatre.

Izzy never stopped talking about the forthcoming Derby to be held on Wednesday, 1st June. She had often seen the horse galloping on the downs and Bert Yates, Ethel's father, knew the lad who rode him every day. She begged her father to take her to see the race. One evening she said, "Dada dear, please, please can we go? Everybody goes. 'April' is going to win, I just feel it. I know it's a funny name for a boy horse but did you know he was called that because he was born on the same day as his breeder? And April the 5th is Mummy's birthday too! Please say we can go." Archie asked her why she thought the horse would win and she answered, "Lucky told me. I asked him…and he nodded!" (Oh dear, I think I was just swaying a bit to some music as she happened to ask me.) As nothing would deter her, he agreed they could walk to the racecourse on the downs from their village, take a picnic and have a day out to witness the great race.

Grace knew that it was traditional for gypsies to make the journey to Epsom every summer to attend Derby week, a chance to meet up with relatives. The fun-fair and Show-Out Sunday were colourful events that drew hundreds of travellers to the downs, eager to buy and sell their wares. She could not help remembering her happy days teaching Manfri and Sinni back at Oil Drum Alley. She wistfully wondered what had become of them over the past twelve years and whether perhaps they may be among the throng of spectators. She pushed her thoughts to the back of her mind.

Derby day dawned bright and sunny. Huge crowds of over half a million people converged on the famous Epsom Downs. The local horse was not expected to win and remained a good bet, so his many supporters waged whatever they could afford on him. Even Archie, swept along by the excitement, put a few shillings on him. April the Fifth ran magnificently. With the crowds screaming and cheering, he came through from the back of the field to storm up the hill to the finishing post and won the biggest race of the year. The public went crazy, parties sprung up everywhere, people scrambled to collect their winnings and it seemed everyone was celebrating.

When Archie went back to collect the profits of his wager from the course, he left Grace and Izzy standing by a tree, sheltered from the mayhem of the crowds. They waited for him near the woods and path that led them back to their village, two miles away. It was quieter there and not far from a few brightly painted wagons belonging to some gypsy families who had come for the festivities. Izzy was fascinated by these and the gaudily decorated pony carts by their side. Several brown and white cobs with long manes and tails were tethered nearby. She couldn't resist going closer but like a true horsewoman, approached them quietly to see if they would let her talk to them. Grace smiled as she watched her horse-mad daughter when a soft deep voice spoke from behind her. "Is that Miss Grace? T'is me, Manfri, come t'see if me yoks (eyes) wer deceivin'me!" She spun round to see a tall, swarthy, tousled-haired man she instantly recognised as her former young student. They hugged joyously and with great excitement Grace introduced Izzy to Manfri who commented on her love of horses, which he'd been quick to spot. When Archie returned, pockets bulging with his winnings, they invited Manfri to walk home with them so they could catch up on each other's news. As they neared the cottage, Manfri said tentatively, "Can I ask, Miss… has you still got me liddle hoss, Bokky?" Grace smiled reassuringly and answered, "What do you think? Come in and see for yourself." Izzy looked puzzled, but her mother told her to wait till they were all indoors and then she'd explain everything.

I was utterly delighted to see Manfri again after so many years. He came to sit by me after giving me a knowing wink and whispered in my ear in his Romany tongue, something like, "Hello my old friend, I see you're as happy as a pony in a pasture!" Manfri related his news; he and his wife still lived with Jed and the Lovells. He had learned the art of roof thatching and business was thriving. Sinni had married, gone to live with her husband's family and had a little boy named Roybin. She had taken up decorating objects in a specialised folk art style, which sold very well to the 'gorjers' (non-gypsies). They still had Hovis, but he was living with Sinni and her young child and was well-loved and happy. Everyone seemed to be prosperous and content with their lives. It was the perfect end to a perfect day. What could possibly go wrong?

CHAPTER 9 'TINASH'

"There is sufficiency in the world for man's need, but not for man's greed." – **Mahatma Gandhi.**

1939

At the start of that year, everything seemed perfect. I had found my 'home for life'. But by the end of the year everyone in Britain had been thrown into turmoil, panic and grief. Now that I am wiser, I have learned there is no such thing as a 'forever' home and when happiness is found, it may only be transient.

Since that wonderful day of the 1932 Derby, our happy family had grown in strength and number. Grace and Archie had a son, an unexpected baby who was welcomed with surprise and pleasure. Isabel adored her baby brother but was busy with her own life; she had excelled in her exams and was working towards becoming a teacher, following in her mother's footsteps. She studied hard during the week and pursued her other passion at weekends. Her love of horses had not diminished; in fact, she had become a proficient horsewoman who was allowed to ride the racehorses out on exercise with the racing lads. Bert Yates, Ethel's father, had coached both girls until they had proved more than capable. It was most unusual to see young women in the male-dominated racehorse industry in those days, so they knew they would have to be content with weekend rides only, and follow more traditional occupations.

Then everything changed. There had been uneasy rumours about another war looming. Most people tried to shrug it off, thinking no Government would commit again to the awful carnage of the last war. As the summer of 1939 drew to an end, it appeared the obsessive greed of one German leader was forcing the hands of many countries to join together to defeat this tyrant. In the September of that year, Britain declared war on Germany. I was terrified. Unlike Izzy, I had lived through the horrors of the First World War. I had seen the desperate destruction and desolation it had brought to our nation. I was scared for Izzy and her young brother. The Smyths were only too aware of what war meant for the country and Archie, when he was a young man, had already served in one war.

A plan was formulated for Izzy to go with Ethel and her family to rural Newmarket in Suffolk as a safety precaution. The Epsom racehorses, their trainer and staff were re-locating there. Many London children were being evacuated for their own safety, sent off into the unknown to live with strangers in distant unfamiliar places. London had learned a harsh lesson in the last war and wished to keep as many youngsters far away from the capital as possible. It must have been a heart-breaking decision for parents to make.

For once I wasn't being forgotten; Izzy refused to leave without me and sought permission for me to be taken with her. Ethel's father Bert worked for the Irishman and Epsom trainer Jack Killadee. Being a jovial, kindly man who thought the world of his two trainee 'lasses', he agreed that I could be brought along. Jack visited the Smyths at Brambler Cottage to discuss important travel and accommodation plans for Izzy's transfer to Newmarket. It had been decided that the girls would live with Ethel's family and would apply to join the local Woman's Land Army once there. This was an organisation formed to recruit a workforce of young women, strong and healthy enough to undertake the agricultural labour needed on British farms for vital food production. If accepted, they would be put to work to replace the labourers who had gone to war. Both girls wanted to do their bit for their country and weren't afraid of hard manual toil. Before Jack left the Smyths, he caught sight of me and whistled softly through his teeth. "Is dat the fellah I'll be takin'? Now dat's what I call a king among rocking horses! Be Jayzus, he's the split image of me first ever racin' pony, 'Tinash'. Oi'll be making good use o' him, mind! He can earn his keep teachin' me apprentices how to sit pretty!" So I proudly became a part of the racing community, off to Newmarket to do 'my bit' during the war.

"Work apace, apace, apace, apace; honest labour bears a lovely face." – **Thomas Dekker.**

1940 saw me settled in a new home, the lodging hall of an old racing yard in Newmarket. Now I had reached the age of 40, I thought I would have developed a tougher heart. If anything, I worried more and grieved harder. I think my past experiences made me aware of what could happen in life and the great sadness events could bring. But putting my fears aside, my spirits were kept up because I was surrounded by cheerful, hopeful and enthusiastic youngsters. Youth brings such infectious joy. I didn't want my dark thoughts about the war to influence these innocent hearts so I pushed anxiety to the back of my mind. Izzy and Ethel came daily to see me and the lads they'd befriended. They had been provisionally accepted by the WLA, but had to wait a few months until they were officially 17 years old. In the meantime they were ecstatic to be allowed to look after and exercise the horses.

I was now officially known as Tinash and I gave serious riding lessons to several apprentice jockeys. Only 13 or 14 years old, some had come from big cities and had never even sat on a horse before. Many had only been sent into the industry by their parents because they were undersized, deemed too weak to ever be capable of doing the work of a full-grown man when older. They were all as light as a sack of feathers! Jack would come and do the instructing himself. I think the young lads enjoyed their time with me, often giving me silly nicknames, which was a sort of racing tradition (you might know someone for years without knowing their real name!). I was called Tin-Tin, Skinny Tinny, and if anyone fell off me, I was Ash the Crash. Really, I was there to teach balance. It was easy work for me and I tried to help them practise by employing certain tricks I'd learned in the past.

One particular tiny lad, aptly nicknamed Sparrow, was very wobbly and unsure as he tried to do various exercises whilst astride me. To strengthen his legs, he was instructed to fold his arms and stand up in his stirrups while I rocked back and forth. I really liked him and tried very hard to give him confidence. Poor Sparrow was homesick and was often bullied by another small but tough cockney lad. This boy had too much cheek. Known as Guttersnipe or Snipey, he would get the others to gang up against Sparrow and make his life a misery. I felt I should intervene and devised a plan to bring Snipey down a couple of pegs. One afternoon, showing off in front of an audience, Guttersnipe was astride me performing the exercise called 'Round the world'. He decided to make it more challenging by placing his hands on his head. This manoeuvre involved swivelling around on my saddle to face sideward, backwards and then to the front again, all done at a sedate rocking pace. It was quite a hard thing to do but he did have excellent balance and would have impressed his little gang of bullies. Success depended entirely on timing. He had to swing his leg over my neck or rump at just the precise moment I was parallel to the ground. I know it was wicked but I couldn't resist, and swung my weight back violently in a half-rear as his leg was completing the final neck swing. Poor Snipey slipped inelegantly backwards over my quarters to end up in the 'gutter'. He was not hurt and leapt to his feet sheepishly among laughing taunts of "Ash the Crash has buried yer good n' proper!" I'd done my job. His pride and ego had taken a bashing and you don't return quickly from falling off a mere rocking horse! When Jack heard about the afternoon's antics, he said thoughtfully, "Now daire's a funny 'ting... Me ole' pony Tinash knew just how t' teach a boy a lesson. He'd do d'very same 'ting to an over-cocky lad!"

So, 1940 saw Izzy and Ethel enlisted into the Women's Land Army and they were sent to work on a nearby farm. The job entailed many long hours of hard labour: looking after pigs, hay-making, controlling vermin and even sawing timber to mend fences. They even learned to drive a tractor! They would return every evening quite exhausted, but they had each other and Izzy was living among dear friends. She certainly missed her family and wrote them many letters, telling them of her life away from home. As the war gathered momentum, Izzy began to realise the seriousness of it all and the danger everyone was in, especially those living in the London area. She fretted about her parents and brother, coming to sit by me for comfort. Izzy would read newspapers or listen to the radio and would tell me all the latest developments. She cut out news articles she'd read and carefully rolled them up and posted them into my belly, through my pommel hole. She refused to call me Tinash; to her I would always be Lucky. "I want you to keep these safe, Lucky, so in the future people can know how absolutely horrid this war is. When they read all these dreadful stories, they may decide to never ever have another war." She was heart-broken when she heard her beloved father Archie Smyth was called up again, despite his age. It seemed so unfair; it would be the second time he was expected to fight for his country, but this time leaving behind a wife and two children.

1945. I don't want to make you too sad, as sad and exhausted as I was by the end, but believe me, that war was worse than anything you can imagine. They called it World War 2, as if there might be more of them. I certainly hope there will never be another event that involved so many nations and brought so much suffering to the world. This was the hardest and longest war ever fought. More men and horses were killed than before. Air raid shelters had been built to try and protect people from the many bombs that rained down on the country. Many different types of missiles had struck us relentlessly. The flying bombs were called doodlebugs or buzz bombs because they had wings and flew over like giant insects. Zeppelin attacks continued to decimate London. Later, rocket bombs had come in droves and were so deadly because they made no warning noise. People were issued gas masks to protect them from deadly gas attacks. Everything was rationed, as Britain was running out of fuel and food for man and beast. Eventually we heard the announcement we had all prayed for. Britain had won the war…but at a very great cost.

I'd been through a war before, but somehow this time it was worse. So many people I knew had been killed. Some were badly wounded or maimed, only to come back to the tragedy of broken families. Although dear Archie returned home, he was a changed man. Suffering from shell-shock which was now termed 'combat stress' or 'battle fatigue', his life was ruined. Living through two world wars had taken its toll. He constantly re-lived the horrific events he'd witnessed and retreated into a private world of terrifying nightmares. Both Grace and Izzy were powerless to reach him. Eventually he was sent away for treatment at a sanatorium.

My dear friends Manfri and Sinni, to whom I owed my life, had also felt the effects of those terrible years. Manfri was luckier than some and although seriously wounded during the final year of the war, managed to return to the New Forest. But Sinni's husband and several of her in-laws were killed on the battlefield, leaving her and her young son Roybin struggling on their own. She made the decision to go home and live with Manfri and the Lovells in the Forest, only to learn that her adored Uncle Jed had also passed away. It was a time of great sadness throughout the country.

"Always think tomorrow will be a better day."

1946. Early in the year, we all came back from Suffolk. Jack Killadee's older staff, who had been called up, returned to their former roles within the yard. Racehorses and staff settled into their old stables in Epsom and I ended up living in the trainer's own house, which was quite a privilege. The house was attached to the stables looking out over the yard. I was installed in the back parlour by the window, giving me a wonderful view of the busy stables. Jack had grown fond of me and loved showing me off to his racehorse owners who came to visit. Izzy and Ethel, now the closest of friends, had something else in common: they had both fallen in love during the war. Ethel met her returning soldier and they had married. Izzy had formed a very close friendship with an Irish jockey lad called Alec, who worked for Jack. They had spent a lot of time together in Newmarket before he was sent to fight. Now back in Epsom, Alec had secured lodgings with his trainer in our house by the yard, so I got to know him and saw Izzy whenever she came to visit. They would come to sit by me on the deep window seat which looked out onto the yard. As they chatted, Alec made a shrewd observation. "You're uncommonly fond of that ole rocker Tinash…" Izzy answered, "You mean Lucky? Yes, of course I am. I've known him all my life! You do realise he's mine really, and Mummy's before that. Jack only borrowed him through the war because I couldn't bear to leave him behind. You could say he's an old friend I've known since I was born…and, well…he's rather different." She wasn't sure if he'd understand just how different I actually was, but his answer reassured her. "I used to teach the apprentices on him when the Guvnor was busy, so I DO know he has a strange way about him. He seemed to know the character of each of those lads, who to help and who to set straight and to teach some manners to! He's a wise ole horse, for sure…"

Izzy and Alec made a lovely couple, but both were pursuing a career and didn't intend to get married quite yet. The country would take a while to recover and rationing was still in place. Izzy had returned to live with Grace and her brother, but they were now in Epsom, renting a tiny house called Folly Cottage. They had been forced to sell their old home and business when Archie went away for treatment. Izzy travelled daily to her college where she was doing a teacher training course. Racing was slowly returning to how it had been before the war, although money was still tight. Alec was a promising jockey and was offered plenty of rides in races. Even though everyone was struggling, he was determined to save whatever he could for their wedding and a future together.

During the war years, the famous Downs and racecourse had suffered damage. At least the sacred gallops where the horses were exercised were spared the irreparable damage that would have been caused if they had been ploughed up and sown with wheat to feed the nation. The Grandstand had been partially destroyed by bombing; there were bomb-craters in the parade rings and several planes had crash-landed on the actual course, despite huge ditches being dug in the chalk all around the area to prevent German crafts from landing. The clean-up was undertaken with gusto. Everyone wanted their pride and joy, their world-famous racecourse, back in full working order. Soon after re-building, exciting news came for the town. It was declared that my favourite race of all time, the Derby, would return to its original home of Epsom Downs. This race belonged at Epsom and just hadn't been quite the same since being re-located to Newmarket through the war years.

On Thursday the 6th of June at 3.30 pm, the 1946 Derby would once again be held on its rightful racecourse. I wasn't surprised at the fuss and excitement this news caused to all the yards and inhabitants of Epsom. It would return to being an important racing town once more. After the gloom and doom of recent years, everyone wanted a reason to celebrate and this was the perfect excuse. A real carnival spirit prevailed before the big day.

Excitement mounted in Jack's little yard and the whole place was given a spruce-up. We were being honoured by an illustrious four-legged guest. One of the best three-year-old colts in the country, a horse entered to run in the race, was coming to lodge with us! In those days, before the advent of fast horse-box transport, racehorses travelled by train. It was traditional for Derby runners to be brought to Epsom a few days early, so they could settle in and relax before the big event. Our yard, being near both the town's station and the downs, was an ideal choice of stabling. News of the horse spread through word of mouth among the lads. His name was Airborne (he had been born in the midst of the war) and he was trained by a friend of Jack's from Newmarket, Dick Perryman. Considered an outsider in the race, he was not expected to win as he was up against stiff competition. It was like 'déjà vu' for me. I'd lived through this very scenario before and wonderful memories of April the Fifth's 1932 Derby flooded over me. Could this be another day of surprises? Can lightning strike twice? They say not, but I've learned over the years that fact is stranger than fiction.

"Some people wait so long for their ship to come in, their pier collapses." – **John Goddard.**

Two days before the big race, Airborne arrived in style with an entourage of staff to care for him. Luckily for me, I had a splendid view of everything that went on in the yard from Jack's parlour window. The small crowd of excited stable boys were stationed ready to welcome the new arrival. His lad, who had walked him so carefully up from the train station, now proudly entered our gates and showed him off in the middle of the yard. Everybody gasped. I felt goose-bumps under my paint and varnish—Goodness me, Airborne looked just like me! He was the most beautiful animal; a tall, elegant, grey thoroughbred with a fine head, arched neck and long slender legs and – can you believe it – he was exactly the same colour as me! This extended to every detail, even the white socks, smokey black knees and hocks merging into pale grey upper legs. His dapples were so similar to mine, clear and bright at first, fading into pale circles as they reached his belly, neck and head. His mane and tail were of mixed dark grey and silver hairs, just like mine. A shiver went down my back and I tried to stop myself feeling foolish pride at our similarity, but then my old friend Sparrow exclaimed loudly what the others were thinking. "Bloomin' jeepers alive! He's the very spit of our ole Tinash, it's his double, I'd swear he's just walked out the Guvnor's house!" The lads were slapping each other on the back, laughing and saying that this was a lucky omen and they all decided they would place a huge wager on Airborne to win the big race.

"Goodness, Airborne looked just like me!"

My uncanny resemblance to Airborne had certainly not gone unnoticed. Dick and Jack had laughed about it the evening before the big day, as they sat in the trainer's house gazing at me and enjoying a nightcap. In racing circles, it was considered an insult for a racehorse to be compared to a rocking horse, insinuating a lack of speed. But Dick assured his host he had total faith that Airborne would win the Derby. Izzy and Alec were amazed at the similarity between the two of us and Alec was determined to put a plan into action. As always, I was in on this secret and I listened as they sat huddled together next to me by the window. He informed Izzy that he had substantial savings hidden away in his room which he intended to use by placing a large bet on our stable guest. She was hesitant, but he argued that this was his chance to win some money towards their future. He quoted sayings such as 'Fortune favours the bold' and 'Faint heart never won fair lady', telling her to have faith in his plan. Alec whispered that he'd heard important information from the lad who rode Airborne and knew the horse well. He had told Alec that the horse raced best when the ground was softened by rain. Finally, he convinced Izzy by asking what she called her little rocking horse. "Lucky," she said and followed the answer with a slow smile and a nod of approval. "But please, Alec, don't go too mad…" she pleaded. Nevertheless, she couldn't help remembering that wonderful day when April the Fifth had thrilled everyone all those years ago.

Derby day dawned cold and wet, not that it dampened anyone's spirits. I glimpsed out of the window and caught sight of Alec happily splashing through a puddle on his way to work, smiling as he looked up at the relentless summer rain and grey clouds. Soon, all the yard work was done and everybody was ready to make their way up to the Downs. Grace was meeting up with her daughter and Alec. She had arranged a lovely surprise for Izzy at a public house on the way. This establishment bore the name of a past Derby winner, Amato, and had a rather special wishing well in its garden. Traditionally and according to local folklore, every year a gypsy would predict the winner of the big race and scribble the horse's name on the wishing well with a piece of Epsom chalk.

When they arrived at The Amato, the crowds had already built up. With half a million people expected to attend this glorious outing, it was becoming impossible to move. Gracie was unable to locate her surprise visitor. Then she spotted a bent twig and grasses pointing towards the back of the building's garden. She mysteriously dragged her daughter down a path towards a shadowy figure. Standing there was Manfri, grinning from ear to ear but looking a little older, with greying hair and a distinct limp. They hugged and laughed, Manfri congratulating Grace for seeing his signs. Izzy excitedly asked him who he thought would win the Derby. He returned her question with one of his own. "How's me liddle hoss Bokki? I hears you has his double running in the race an' he likes a bit o wet ground! Wotda YOU think will win?" and he winked at Alec. Before they left to walk up to the Downs, Izzy pushed her way through the crowd to see what had been written on the well. There, scrawled in white letters was the name AIRBORNE. She ran back to tell them and asked Manfri if he believed the old tale. Manfri just winked again and quietly produced a small lump of chalk from his pocket which he then threw into the hedgerow.

Now I will tell you about the strange thing that happened to me that day. Everyone had gone to watch the race and I was left in the house, resigned to the fact that I must wait patiently to hear the outcome. At 3.30 that afternoon I must have dozed off – unlikely as I was so excited, but there's no other explanation. I had a crazy dream that I was rocking as fast as I've ever rocked before in my life. My heart was thudding, I could feel that silky soft turf beneath my feet, my lungs were bursting with the sheer exhilaration of speed. Faster and faster I rocked, my breath coming in huge gulps as I drank in the air. I could hear the crowd roar and I had never felt so alive. My rocking slowed and I must have woken up, but it was so vivid. I still can't explain the damp feeling of sweat on my varnish or why my mane was so tangled and wind-swept after that surreal experience. Anyway, I still had to wait to find out what had actually happened on that memorable Derby day.

Well the rest, as they say, is history. The Royal family was in attendance, waving to the multitude of people who had spent their last pennies to be there. Everyone had been given a day off work. It was to be enjoyed as a well-deserved holiday, a celebration to mark the end of the war. Just before the race, the rain stopped and the sun shone down on the seventeen horses lined up at the start. Airborne was near the back of the field most of the way round until his jockey nudged him on in the straight. He loved the rain-soaked turf under his feet and took off like a rocket. After gliding effortlessly passed all his competitors as they started to tire in the soft ground, he hit the front and won easily. The crowds erupted with joy, grey horses were always popular with the public and a lot of people had won a lot of money.

All special days are precious and this was another of those I'll always remember. A great yard party awaited the staff when the victorious horse returned. Airborne was treated like a king, rubbed down, watered, fed and left to rest. Everyone then retired to Jack's house for a celebratory drink. I was the centre of attention that evening. Everybody patted and slapped my back, calling me 'Little Airborne' or 'Airborne's lucky mascot', and lifted their glasses to toast me as a winner. It was all rather wonderful as everyone I cared about had won hundreds of pounds – a real fortune in those days. Before the evening ended, Alec came to me with a fond smile, deftly raised the flap of my saddle and dropped a small, tightly folded scrap of paper through the pommel hole which wafted gently into my belly. He whispered softly in my ear, "I'll propose to her tomorrow." I knew not what was on that little piece of paper, but I would keep it safe for him and it would be our secret.

Before Airborne left the next day to return to Newmarket, his special lightweight racing shoes called 'plates' were removed by the farrier and replaced with normal iron shoes. Jack's head-lad Bert saved one as a memento. This was a ritual done by the yards lucky enough to lodge a Derby winner. That aluminium plate was then mounted on blackened tin and inscribed with neat white script. As was the tradition, the plaque was then nailed to the door of the stable where the horse had stayed. Airborne's plaque joined two others in our yard; that of Sansovino's from the 1924 Derby and Hyperion's from 1933.

My next few years were full of joy, as memories of the war became less painful. Archie returned home to the love and care of his family. Ethel and Izzy remained the best of friends, both now happily married with their own children. Alec had used his winnings wisely. He had secured a little property for his new family in a nearby village and continued to work at the racing stables. I lived a contented life in Jack's house, often visited by my dear friends. Of course, I was in my element when the two girls brought their toddlers round to visit. Once again I was back to doing what I did best, teaching Izzy and Ethel's two babes, Mirabel and Edward, how to ride. But as I have learned from the past, all good things rarely last and I'm sorry to say, my life then took a downward turn…yet again.

Chapter 10 'Zeppelin'

1950

This was a tragic year when everything in my life changed for good, or should I say, for the worse. At fifty years of age, my life was all I could have hoped for. I was safe and content, watching life in the yard unfold daily from my view through the window. Recently, I'd noticed that the annual stable spring clean was extending to a re-paint of the whole yard. The Derby plaques were carefully removed from their stable doors and brought into the house for safe-keeping. Woodwork received a new coat of green paint and the flint walls were given a bright application of whitewash.

Then calamity struck. Our lovely trainer was up a ladder, mending a light I think, but I only remember the awful sight that I witnessed through that parlour window. The ladder slipped and he crashed to the ground and lay there, quite still. I was frozen to the spot as I watched and heard the anguished cries of everyone rushing to help him. He was carefully lifted on to a horse rug improvised as a stretcher and carried into the house. Doctors came and went but we never saw Jack in the yard again. I never even saw him in the house, as he lay upstairs with dreadful injuries to his head. A gloomy mood descended upon the yard, but the staff continued as best they could. After a few weeks the trainer had not improved; then a grim atmosphere pervaded the house as the doctor made his final visit and announced that Jack had died during the night.

It was a huge funeral with many people lining the road to watch the horse-drawn hearse make its way up to the cemetery. On their return, people dressed in dark clothes filed into Jack's house to pay their respects. All my old friends were present: Grace, Archie and their son, Ethel and Izzy with their families. Even dear Manfri came and was a huge comfort to all. The staff and owners were sombre and I heard so many quiet sobs coming from every corner of the parlour. It felt so strange, as that house had always been such a cheerful, happy place. Our jovial guvnor had gone, and nothing would ever be the same again. It wasn't long before everything was packed away and removed from the house. As had happened once before in my life, the workmen who cleared the house, took me outside and I trembled at the thought of what they might do with me. Luckily I was placed in the old feed store. I have to say, they were kind and careful with me, even throwing one of the discarded tatty exercise rugs over me for protection. This small consideration gave me comfort, but I did wonder what had been planned for my future. Not knowing my fate was simply torture. Yet again I found myself alone, confused and abandoned, gazing out of a small grubby window onto an empty yard. No clopping of hooves, banging of doors, clanking of buckets—just silence. Both horses and staff had gone to other yards. The equipment, stables and house were all up for sale. The place was deserted…and I had been forgotten.

"A liar needs a good memory." – **Anon.**

Days later, I had a visit from one of the workmen and his son. I heard the main gate being unlocked and they entered rather surreptitiously. At first I was delighted to see them, imagining they had come to take me to my friends, but their conversation sent shivers through me. It became clear they were dishonest and had a plan to kidnap me to make some money for themselves. The father whispered, "Lor', he's still 'ere. They ain't picked him up yet. Bit o' luck fer us then, son." The lad answered, "Leave it to me, Dad. Me 'an the lads'll nab him tonight an' take him to Uncle Gordon's winter yard. Should git a few bob for him, eh!" They smiled craftily and crept out of the place, locking up behind them. I was in turmoil; I couldn't move or hide and had no way of escaping before tonight, when I would be stolen. My mind was racing with thoughts of past experiences. I'd been in tight spots before and I'd always managed to form a plan. Then it became clear to me what I should do…but I hadn't needed to call on my old gypsy trick for so long, I was not sure it would work. Concentrating on knowing I had the lucky twig and little carved flower in my belly, I thought hard of Manfri, picturing his face and begging him for help… But my luck had run out. That night, I was bundled into a van driven by two men who sneaked into the yard under the cover of darkness and drove me away to goodness knows where.

Manfri awoke in the middle of the night from a disturbing nightmare. His wife tried to comfort him but he was inconsolable. He paced around until dawn broke. Then he was off to a neighbour who had a telephone. "Grace, sorry 'tis so early, but I needs to know if me dear liddle hoss is safe! Is Bokky wiv you an' Archie?" Grace sounded a bit blurry at being woken so early but told Manfri she was sure Izzy and Alec had picked me up from Jack's yard, once the place was cleared after the funeral. Manfri was still not convinced, he'd dreamt that I was in deep trouble and he'd sensed my panic. The next phone call he made to Izzy, confirmed his worst fears. She told Manfri that no, her parents must have picked me up during that week because when she and Alec went to bring me home, I was gone. They'd looked in the house and yard and then had given the keys back to the selling agent, presuming I was safe with the Smyths. They hadn't been at all worried because the whole place had been securely locked. The silence on the end of the line sent a chill down Izzy's spine. Finally Manfri said in a strange hard voice, "Dordi, dordi, dordi, (Oh dear, oh dear) our liddle Bokki has been chored (stolen). He AIN'T wiv yer Ma…"

Of course, I knew nothing of this and I'm afraid to say, I felt hurt and disillusioned that no one seemed to care what fate befell me. Little did I know how distraught they were or how hard they tried to find me. Manfri was like a man possessed. He travelled up from the Forest and made a huge effort in his search. He threatened the agent, telling him it could only have been his men and to expect trouble if the theft was not cleared up. The police were informed but had little interest, scoffing that I was only a toy horse of little value. Manfri knew he'd have to do his own brand of investigating. Through contacts among the settled gypsy folk around Epsom, he got the name of a fellow who did house-clearance work, had relations who were fairground people and they owned a funfair business. This name tallied with a man who had worked for the selling agency. After trying to lie about their employee, Manfri forced the agent to reveal an address for this scoundrel. Eventually the company admitted the yard keys had been returned late, giving the suspected man ample opportunity to steal me.

A visit was made to the villain's house and when faced with the angry gypsy knocking on his door, the man tried to deny he'd even worked for the agent. Unfortunately for him, his son gave the game away as he appeared from inside, to defend his father. "We don't know nothing about the spotted rockin' horse, the place was empty when we left it." Manfri was furious. Their slip-up had exposed them as liars but still, they would admit to nothing. In desperation, he threatened to place a 'curse' on the pair and despite a punch on the nose for the son, he could get no solid proof of the theft. The only information he managed to extract from the nervous father was vague. He'd muttered that I was probably miles away by now with some fair, doing the rounds up and down the country. It was something, but not enough for Manfri to actually locate me. But he never stopped looking.

Archie put out feelers in the antique business. It had been years since he was involved with rocking horses but he still knew the names of people who bought and sold us. With a detailed description of me, a hefty reward and even a photograph, I was on a shortlist of horses that had been stolen. All the dealers were on the look-out for me but alas, I was not in those circles and was never found. The Smyths were desolate at their loss, Izzy grieved for me as if she'd lost a brother. Manfri's family, Sinni and her boy Roybin and all the New Forest folk who'd heard about me were devastated that I had been so cruelly snatched when my people had been in mourning. It was a low trick that would never be forgiven. Whether it was due to a 'curse' or not, that man and his son seemed to have a continuous run of very bad luck for many years after the event.

"Resilience can be measured by how quickly one is able to recover."

1953. I don't want to harp on about how miserable my life has been since being kidnapped, because I have survived and after three years, I'm still here to tell the tale. But it was not a happy one at first. After a long, cold journey, I found myself in some kind of large workshop. I was unloaded and placed next to various strange creatures that seemed to be modelled out of a hard material, certainly not wood. More disturbingly, some of them were not even whole. Beasts were lying about with no heads or legs, some huge birds had wings missing. It was like being in a nightmare animal hospital. At least they were not real, so I wasn't scared as they could do me no harm. But I was lonely and confused. I almost wished one of them would come to life and tell me where I was and why I was being kept prisoner.

Imagine how I jumped when I heard a soft, low, velvet-toned voice coming from a shadowy corner. It was the purr of a cat. I'd met cats at Oil Drum Alley and in the racing yard, but never conversed with one before. This one must have read my thoughts because he started to explain in a casual manner, that we were in the winter quarters of a large funfair firm called Mauler and Sons and this was the repair shop for broken 'rides'. Stalking around, looking me up and down, he assessed me knowingly and predicted I'd soon be transformed into a 'mount'. He noted my leg position was that of a 'jumper' but he couldn't make up his mind if I'd be part of the Galloping Horses or the Wild Creatures roundabout. No, he said, I wasn't quite right to be a 'galloper'; I just didn't have the look of a carousel horse or a wild animal for that matter. I'd probably be turned into a mount to go on the War Horses. This, he elaborated, was a roundabout made up of various horses and mules modelled on famous equine heroes of the two World Wars. They were painted with wings on their bodies, to represent aeroplanes flown during the war. Each was named after a clever British military deception strategy used to trick the Germans, which had helped us to win. Then he rambled on about how dated the ride was nowadays, as the war was years ago and nobody would remember or even care about how we actually managed to win.

This cat didn't speak with words, but I understood everything through his rather vocal purring. He introduced himself as the owner of the workshop and was known as Diesel. Apparently, when he was a tiny kitten, he had fallen into a bucket of the vile liquid. Even though he'd been washed thoroughly, no one thought he'd survive but he proved them wrong. He was then placed in the building and told, "Diesel, this is now YOUR workshop, remember you're the boss. No vermin!" Being an imposing, large and handsome ginger tom with sparklingly clean white markings, there was definitely an air of being 'in charge' about him. He certainly seemed to know everything that happened here.

A few days passed and I must admit I was thankful for that cat. Diesel was a comfort, perched on my saddle, chatting away to no one in particular. He would periodically leave me to do his 'rounds'. He stalked off one morning to return with some news. "They're coming to do you today. Don't worry, I'll be here to oversee the work." Well, he was right as usual. First, my swing-stand was removed, for the second time in my life. Then I was lifted onto a workbench surrounded by tins of paint and tools. This was nothing like my original Maker's workshop because I found myself straddled across the bench but this time, horror of horrors, I was to be stripped down. The men who worked on me were not craftsmen who took care to produce something they were proud of, but just Mauler's employees, working to a schedule to get me transformed hurriedly to replace a broken horse on their roundabout.

Diesel watched the proceedings in a matter-of-fact way, washing himself all the while. My saddle and bridle were removed, my mane and tail sheared off to a mere couple of inches. But worse to come, my whole body was covered in cold oily white paint. You know how proud I used to be of my dapples, so you can imagine how gut-wrenching this felt. Later when I had dried, the men decorated me with huge thick eyelashes, a circus-red colour on parts of my face, bright orange, yellow and red flames all over my body and then they painted strange large wings on my flanks. I think Diesel could sense my indignation because he purred harshly under his breath, "Don't moan, it could have been worse. At least I persuaded them to do you in 'ginger and white'. You could have ended up purple."

To add insult to injury, my lovely old leather tack was replaced with a scarlet-coloured plastic saddle and bridle. They gave me a new name, scrolled across my neck in decorative gold and navy blue paint. The men went home, satisfied with their handiwork. I was left to dry overnight and would be fitted to the roundabout the next day. Up till now I'd said nothing, but I couldn't resist asking Diesel what name had been written on me. "Zeppelin, of course. The other Zeppelin chappie broke a leg. He's being patched up at our southern depot, so you've been drafted-in to go with Turpitude, Vendetta, Fortitude and Royal Flush. I told you. You five are named after brilliant deception strategies that foiled the Germans." I had to protest and shouted in desperation, "But I'm a quality rocking horse, NOT a mere fairground carousel mount or a galloper or any old funfair ride or whatever I've been turned into! It's just not right. It's UNFAIR!" Diesel was not impressed with my outburst and growled some home truths back at me. He told me not to be a snob. I should be honoured to be representing the noble efforts of those who helped us win the war. He remarked coldly that times were hard and he was fully aware I was not quite right for the job, but needs must, the show MUST go on and the kiddies must have their funfair. He told me not to be selfish; I should just give the kids their thrills and count my blessings.

These strong words brought me to my senses and I tried to accept my situation with grace. I'd been in worse places before and survived. I must be strong and remember my mantra; I must be kind to the children who ride me. I think the ginger tom felt sorry that he'd been so harsh, because he came to sit with me all night long. I smiled to myself as I listened to him moaning softly about the paint fumes and that he'd preferred the warm leather saddle to this cold plastic one and he jolly well hoped that I would cheer up by the morning. It was hard to feel cheery when the men arrived at dawn and prepared to move me again. As they carried me out, I shouted to Diesel but he calmly answered, "I'll see you soon, mate." A lorry took me a short drive away to the nearby village green where the funfair was being erected. Here I met my future

I wore my new name 'Zeppelin' with pride.

colleagues, the War Horses, who would work with me giving children's rides for the unforeseeable future. The fairground boys attached me to the roundabout's ceiling with an ornate golden spiralled pole that was securely fitted into my pommel hole. I was now officially part of a themed merry-go-round and was locked in servitude, probably for the rest of my life. My new identity was now 'Zeppelin'. I don't know about merry-go-round, I felt it should be re-named misery-go-round. It was hard to feel cheery.

"Forgiveness is the fragrance the violet sheds on the heel that has crushed it." – **Mark Twain**

Believe it or not, my mood and spirits rose considerably during the next week. I started to actually enjoy the company of the lovely children who flocked excitedly to our circular platform to ride us. It took me a while to accustom myself to the strange up and down action of this ride, which gave so much pleasure to my little jockeys. Also, I had to get used to the garishly loud organ music which blared out old tunes that had been sung by many throughout the war years. The parents loved it and sang along with the organ as they waited for us to slow down so they could collect our riders. My glass eyes had to adjust to the bright coloured bulbs, flashing lights and myriad mirrors reflecting the vivid paintwork within the carousel. At first it was a crazy assault on my senses, but surprisingly soon, I began to feel the joy of it all. Everyone at the fair seemed so happy; I even got to like the mixed aromas of hotdogs, fried onions and candyfloss that mingled with the pervading smell of crushed grass and industrial oil. The fairground atmosphere was beginning to feel like home.

One night at the end of that first week, I had a visitor. I felt a gentle plonk as he alighted on my saddle and I could feel his warmth radiate onto my back as he curled up with front paws tucked under him.

Diesel had trotted over from the workshop to join me for a chat. I was so pleased to have his company again as I'd been quite lonely. "See you've cheered up a bit. Not all bad, is it, now you've got used to everyone. Made any friends yet?" I explained that nobody here talked but he answered curtly, "How do you know? Have you tried talking to them?" I must admit I had tried but they just weren't like me so we couldn't converse; however, I was really curious about the characters they represented. Diesel, never short of interesting information, gave me chapter and verse on my War Horse companions. Next to me was Turpitude, a mule who represented the amazing work these beasts had undertaken as draught animals in the thick of battle. Vendetta, Fortitude and Royal Flush were in front and slightly behind me and represented the mounts of soldiers that had been faithful to their masters till the last. It was true, we five were named after the 1944 operations of deception utilised by the Government.

Diesel was so clever; I really don't know how he knew these things. Round the corner from me and directly opposite were three really famous horses with their names blazoned across their necks, Regal, Olga and Upstart. Two were in the galloping position and one had two legs on the ground. Instead of flames and wings, they were decorated with garlands and ribbons and a bronze 'Dickin' medal painted on their chests. This was the animal equivalent of the Victoria Cross medal and was awarded for outstanding bravery, gallantry and devotion to duty whilst serving in the Armed Forces. Diesel added that not only horses, but dogs, pigeons and (of course) a cat named Simon had also been awarded the Dickin medal, a huge accolade. Out of my line of vision were two more Dickin medal holders: horses modelled on the First World War heroes, the mare awarded the name Sergeant Reckless, and Warrior, who later became known as 'Joey' in the book and film, 'War Horse'.

I had always hated talking about the war, but this clever cat made the subject so interesting that I was hungry for more information. I never tired of listening to his inspiring tales, his knowledge seemed endless. Once, I asked him how he knew so much about everything and he said simply, "I eavesdrop." Then I asked how he could believe what he heard, as people often lied. He replied, "I know if they're lying. I'm a cat." I do know that Diesel's talks helped me to feel proud to be standing amongst such heroes and from then on, I wore my new name 'Zeppelin' with pride.

"The one thing that can change a victim into a happy survivor is a choice of attitude."

I no longer felt imprisoned, just in service, doing my old job of giving children pleasure. This change of attitude helped me get through the years I was with the fair. Also, I was receiving an education of sorts. You see a wide spectrum of life from a roundabout. I was learning about a facet of life I had no knowledge of before. The culture and history of the travelling showmen of Britain fascinated me and had a certain parallel to that of Romany gypsies. Gypsies thought they were a cut above, having a long history since leaving India and traversing half the world to be here. Their language and culture were unique. Showmen too, had a sort of dialect, a 'fairground jargon' of their own and an unwritten code of conduct. They were a strong clan of travelling people with a network of family businesses all over Britain. A lot of firms had their designated fairground pitches where they returned year after year. Most owned a winter base. Years ago, each firm employed wonderfully skilled carpenters who made the figurines and animals for the rides. This was before newer, cheaper materials were invented. Those clever artists worked their wood, fashioning the original galloping horses for merry-go-rounds, not unlike my Maker. He carved rocking horses, but both could have done either's job. Fairground artists were also talented painters and sign-writers. Their decoration was done in a folk art style of their own, not unlike the type used to decorate barge boats and gypsy living wagons. Of course, Sinni's beautifully painted objects were also in this style.

I had been working on the War Horses for a while, when I had a strange and uplifting encounter with a wizened old man. He must have been around eighty years old and was grandfather to one of the fairground lads, Nelson. This young man often worked on our War Horse ride and was always cheerful and charming to the public. I grew very fond of him. He loved the youngsters, lifting them so gently on and off our backs. Always grinning and chatting away to everyone, he was very popular with the ladies and reminded me of a young Manfri. One morning, while Nelson was busy sponging our saddles clean from the night before, the old man came hobbling up to speak to his grandson. As he was talking, he stopped abruptly mid-sentence and peered intently at me. He asked Nelson to help him clamber onto the platform so he could inspect me closely. "Whatever's this one doing up here, boy?" he demanded. The lad answered, "The old Zeppelin broke, Grand Da. This is the replacement. Why d'ya ask?" His grandfather shook his head and told Nelson that I had no business being here, that I was not a carousel horse at all, but an old rocking horse. He continued that I was not just any old rocker, but a 'Leach' horse, out of one of the smallest but best firms in the country. He started talking excitedly and seemed to be in a trance, as old memories flooded back. "Even under all that paint I can see the quality of him. I reckon I can even tell you who made him. He's got the look of my ole mate Wilf's horses. Always done the head lovely, the eyes is in the right position, see, not too high. An' look at them pasterns, proper nice cut-out heels from fetlock to foot. Oh, he's got 'Wilf' stamped all over him…" By now Nelson had absolutely no idea what his rambling old grandfather was saying and tried to get on with his work. The old man persisted and, grabbing his arm, asked him where I'd come from. Nelson told him that his cousin had 'found' me down south and brought me up to sell to his dad. The old man looked at me with pity in his eyes. He said angrily, "Found? Found? You mean thieved! Shame on your da. Some poor kiddie will have gone to bed crying, that's for sure."

At least someone was aware of what had happened to me! How amazing it felt to be recognised for what I once was. The stooped old man came back to see me several times. I like to think I reminded him of his old friend Wilf and I know I felt close to him for knowing my lovely Maker. I couldn't wait to see Diesel again, to tell him what had happened and ask if he knew anything. Soon, I got my chance and he listened with mild interest saying, "I'll see what I can do." Later, while sitting on my back one night, the ginger cat told me he'd made enquiries about the old man. Apparently, he was known as Albie the Knife and was one of the best woodworkers in the country. As a boy, Albie had been apprenticed to a small but famous London rocking horse factory. After some years he had left there to join the Mauler family's firm where he had taken the job of carving the 'gallopers' for their roundabouts. I told you fact is stranger than fiction!

Chapter 11. 'Zeppy'

"Hold fast to dreams, for if dreams die, life is a broken-winged bird that cannot fly…"

1956

I had been working for Mauler's fair for six years. We'd travelled all over the place doing the same fairground circuit year in year out. Life continued in much the same vein; we rested at the yard for the worst of the winter months and hit the road again in the spring. A travelling fair with its convoy of shiny stainless steel living wagons and lorries loaded with fun-rides, always caused a stir of excitement when it came to town.

When one of the old funfair companies closed down, Mauler and Sons picked up their work and we headed for a new ground. It was a pleasant town, further south than we usually travelled. The lads had set our ride up quickly for evening business in our new location. This night, I was to meet a little girl who, unbeknown to me, would change my life for ever. Compared to all the others who had ridden me on the roundabout, this child was different. Straight away she knew that I was, too. Unlike most children who just climbed aboard any horse that happened to stop nearest to them, this girl took her time in choosing who she wanted to swirl her round. I only noticed her because I kept passing that earnest little face as she stood on the ground next to her mother. She seemed to be studying each of us closely for the few seconds that we flew past. I saw how her face lit up whenever I went by and her eyes followed me till I was out of sight. Several times she tried to find me when we slowed and stopped, dragging along her mother who had a tight hold of her hand. She'd noticed our somewhat faded names and asked her mother to help find me. "Look out for Zepp-something," she pleaded. Each time, I started up again before the pair could reach me. Her mother tried to walk her away to another attraction but the girl's persistence paid off and I eventually slowed down near enough for her to wrench free and run to me.

She leapt on to the platform and grabbed my leg so no one else could claim me. Just before we set off again, Nelson spotted her and ran to swoop the child up, placing her gently on my back. "I take it you wanted to ride Zeppelin, then!" he teased, as he'd seen her determination. "Yes, he's the one I was looking for, only him," she replied softly. The band struck up and off we went. How fearless this little girl was, riding me with total confidence, her small hands stroking my neck, her face near mine as she leaned forward in the saddle. I heard her whisper, "Gosh, you're so pretty, nothing like the others, you feel so real. You're exactly the pony from my dreams."

Her mother ended up having to pay Nelson for three consecutive rides, as the child refused to dismount me. We whizzed round and round, up and down, in our own little world of total delight. It was as if we'd fallen in love with each other. Perhaps she reminded me of Grace or Izzy, maybe it was that I had sorely missed this close relationship with someone who understood me. All I knew was that I never wanted to be parted from her. Love at first ride… for both of us. On our last rotation she promised me she would try to get out secretly later that night and we could escape the roundabout and go for a real ride. "Meet you here later, Zeppy," she said in a hushed tone. It sounded like so much fun but I knew it was an impossible dream and I felt a stabbing pain in my heart. As the roundabout slowed to a halt, Nelson grabbed the child from my back and returned her to her mother who was keen to depart before any more pennies were spent. I watched in despair as she was unwillingly dragged away. I wanted to call out to my little rider so badly that I tried something I'd never done before. I experimented with a neigh. Luckily, I was facing in her direction and despite the jumble of loud music coming from different stalls, the sound of my whinny must have reached her ears. As I gazed at the departing figure, I could hardly believe it: she heard me, pulled back from her mother's grip, turned and blew me a kiss.

What happened later that night was one of the loveliest memories of my life. I honestly didn't think I would ever see that little girl again, yet at midnight she appeared, wrapped up warmly in a navy duffle coat and thick woollen scarf. I heard my name softly whispered as she tip-toed round the platform gazing up at each horse to catch sight of the one she had so diligently chosen. When she found me, her face lit up and like a quick and agile cat, she slipped onto my back, full of energy and excitement.

It defies all reason, but we started to move round, slowly at first then faster till everything became a blur. It was a very windy night which may explain us moving-but how does one explain the changing scenery? Fields and hedges rolled past; then I was galloping down lanes and tracks until I felt the metalled surface of a road under my wooden hooves. Suddenly, we were on a cobbled street in London outside the old Leach workshop. I caught sight of my Maker through that big display window, happily chiselling away at another little horse. I so wanted to tell him I was fine and happy but I couldn't stop; my little rider was urging me on and on. Next, I recognised Kilwick Manor up ahead, but she whispered, "Keep going, Zeppy, till we find somewhere nice." So, on I galloped and we soon reached my old home, the Rectory. At last I pulled myself up to a standstill and she and I gazed through the parlour window at a lovely scene. The whole Tubb family were cheerfully eating their Christmas dinner around their scrubbed pine table. Everything looked as I remembered…but I was not there, in that room. "They look really nice," she said simply, followed with, "come on, let's go. Show me more!"

We seemed to being doing a tour of my life, it was quite extraordinary. I tried to show her all the good parts but we also visited some sad places too. It didn't matter much; it only helped to make the happy times seem even sweeter. She saw Grace and Izzy, Manfri and Sinni, in all the places I'd been with them. I took her to that glorious Derby day and actually saw Airborne win, although I think it was me… She screamed with excitement as I galloped her up the racecourse. After the race, I decided to take her down the lane and show her Jack's yard from where I'd been stolen, but I just couldn't find it. I searched the lanes all around but never found our old stables. Suddenly, we were both gripped with panic as streaks of light appeared in the sky and dawn broke. "Quick, Zeppy, you've got to get us back. Mummy will be waking me for my breakfast soon and the fair boys won't be able to find you..."

Don't ask me how we got home, let alone how we managed the whole night's adventure, but we did make it back in the nick of time. It was a wild, wet and windy morning, still very early. Nelson hadn't yet appeared with his bucket and sponge to clean our saddles and poles. We seemed to be back on the roundabout, rather out of breath and wind-swept from the speed of that ride home. My lovely little friend dismounted gently, looking a bit wobbly as she hugged me quickly and promised that she'd be back after school later that day. She started running home but turned and shouted, "I love you, Zeppy!" I was panicking, I might never see her again and well, I think I loved her too. "I don't even know your name!" I screamed after her. She turned again, smiling and shouted a word back, but it got lost, swirled away in the wind and rain. All I remember was the end of that word, it sounded like lyn or leen. Suddenly knowing her name was THE most important thing in the world; my only chance of keeping her alive in my head.

Diesel appeared from nowhere. He streaked across the sodden grass and shook violently before leaping on my back to perform morning ablutions. He'd been sheltering from the rain under the platform opposite mine. I forgot to mention that this cat came everywhere with us, travelling in the flashiest living wagon with the boy he owned. His lad was called Davey, one of Mauler's sons and the man responsible for his rescue as a kitten, after which they had become inseparable. Of course, a cat like him travelled the country; you didn't acquire knowledge like his by spending all your days in a barn. I was thrilled to see him and was bursting to tell him all about the strange happenings of the previous night.

"Who was that blonde child I just saw running off?" he asked suspiciously, adding, "You're not 'moonlighting' are you?" I didn't understand the question but needed to tell him everything. "Diesel, you'll NEVER believe what happened last night!" I declared. He answered in a bored tone: "Try me."

So I told Diesel the whole story, right from the beginning to the end and waited for a reaction. "You're right. I don't believe you," was his curt answer. He tried to give me a reasonable explanation for the event. He told me that lots of animals on roundabouts tend to 'burn out' after a few years. "It's due to the constant round and round movement. It can turn you crazy – where do you think the expression 'round the bend' came from?" he asked. "Look at your feet, they're all frayed and split, look at your paintwork, it's tired and peeling. Your mind's in a spin. You're suffering 'burn out', mate." I argued and insisted that the events of last night really had happened, but my words were lost on him. He was stalking around, gazing up at the horses around me and looking quite perplexed. "Something's wrong here. You're always next to Turpitude the mule, now you're beside Fortitude. You've moved…I'm off to do some digging, there's got to be a sane explanation to all this nonsense," he growled. Before he left I said sadly that I was heart-broken because I didn't even know her name. He replied kindly, "Well luckily for you, I heard her shout something as she ran off, but I only caught the first bit. Sounded like a boy's name. I think she said Jack-something…" This was exciting because I'd heard the ending, so we pieced it together and worked out her name could be Jack-lyn or Jack-leen. After a moment's thought, Diesel announced with pride, "Got it. She's called Jacqueline, a very popular name these days, mate." I felt so happy and relieved and whispered the name over and over to myself. Jacqueline!

> *"Hold fast to dreams, for when dreams go, life is a barren field frozen with snow."* – **Langston Hughes.**

When he returned hours later, I could see from his sober face that the cat had some news, but it wasn't going to be good. "I think I've solved your mystery, old mate, but you ain't going to like it." He continued to explain that I HAD been off the platform last night, because the workmen had collected both me and Turpitude and taken us to the transport lorry for inspection. The mule had been withdrawn from service due to wear and tear. I was also scheduled for 'retirement', but I'd been returned to the roundabout temporarily, until a spare could be found. This, Diesel said, explained my change of position and my disorientation. "The last thing YOU remember was whizzing round and round with that blonde kid before it scrambled your brains. Anyway, this could be your last night ever. We leave here tomorrow. You'll be relieved of duties, old son. I'm really sorry, mate…I'll miss you – and your crazy dreams."

I can't explain how desolate I felt at that moment. Diesel didn't want an embarrassing show of emotion, so he shot off, but I knew he was upset. I wasn't sure what 'retirement' meant, where I'd end up or what would become of me. More importantly I wondered if I'd ever see my little rider again. She said she would return, so as usual, all I could do was wait. All that afternoon and evening, as I gave my very last rides as a fake carousel horse, I looked frantically around the showground for a small, slim blonde figure, but she never came back.

Early next morning, my dear fair boy Nelson detached me from the ceiling with the others and loaded us in the lorry. Everything was packed up, cleared and tidied in record time. The fair boys worked as a team, they'd had years of practice and were as efficient as a well-oiled machine. Soon we were back on the road, our lorries and showman's wagons making a snake-like convoy as we headed out of town.

Later that afternoon, a little girl looked across the deserted showground with tears streaming down her face. She stood where the roundabout had been, saw the circular imprint in the worn grass and the long muddy furrows where the lorries had driven away – and she wept. After that night out, she had been in so much trouble because her clothes were soaked through. Her mother guessed she'd left the house after dark in the rain, but her daughter refused to say where she'd gone or why. It had been difficult to escape the house after school because of her curfew punishment but when she eventually managed to run to the showground, the awful truth dawned on her. She'd come too late…I was long gone.

Chapter 12 'Icarus'

"He who fears he will suffer, already suffers what he fears." – **Michel de Montaigne**

Rarely had I been at such a low ebb. Fear had overcome me and I'd lost all hope of having any sort of future. What a terrible state I had fallen into both physically and mentally, and I admit I was consumed with self-pity. It was probably many months that I'd lain in Mauler's winter quarters in my 'retired' state. Now I was one of those dying and dismembered beasts I'd seen when I first arrived six years ago. I expect I looked a sorry sight and certainly didn't feel like conversing with Diesel. He had grown tired of my defeatist attitude and just didn't have time for anyone suffering from love-sickness or depression. His visits became less frequent, so I was surprised when he re-appeared one morning with some breaking news. Apparently, a dealer called Mr Pilchard was coming on his yearly visit to acquire unwanted fairground memorabilia. Diesel told me in no uncertain terms to buck myself up, put my bravest face on, cheer up and look lively.

"This is tantamount to an escape plan!" he hissed urgently at me. "Look, son, fail to prepare, prepare to fail. This may be your one and only chance of getting out of here. If you ever want to see your precious Jacqueline again – grab it!"

Oh yes, Diesel was an astute and crafty cat! That was about the only thing he could have said to stir me into action and wrench me out of the doldrums. I'd honestly begun to believe that my strange adventure that night had never happened at all but was merely a symptom of my 'burn-out'. Now, the mention of her name rejuvenated me. There was nothing I could do to change my appearance or position. It looked like my paint-faded wings had failed me and I had crash-landed off the roundabout to lay prone on the barn floor. What had changed was my attitude. I had to believe I would catch the dealer's eye as a valuable fairground piece and that he would take me out of this place.

When Mr Pilchard arrived I had an ally by my side. Nelson's grandfather had come to stand by me, ready to sing my praises as he believed I deserved a better life away from the fair. With heartfelt gratitude I heard him tell the dealer my history, my age and even how valuable I would be in restored condition. Being a seasoned negotiator, the man hid his interest and retorted, "Nah, it would cost me an arm and a leg to get that fellah back to what he should be. We only buy 'wrecks' as decorative pieces and he'll need a lot of work just to get him fit enough to go into someone's front room." The grandfather cleverly answered, "Well then, he's perfect for your needs. He's got great provenance, too." This comment struck a chord with the shrewd man. Although he feigned disinterest by walking away and inspecting many other items, he eventually returned to stand next to me and slapped Mr Mauler's hand to buy me.

I have my Maker's old friend and Diesel to thank for my ticket to freedom. In all the excitement of leaving, I didn't get the chance to say farewell to my old ginger companion. I never realised how very much I would miss him, a true friend who had helped me through thick and thin.

As I left my old fairground life, lying on the floor of their van, I heard the dealer and his partner discussing me in detail. There was no window to spy through, so I decided to take a leaf out of Diesel's book and do some serious eavesdropping of my own. Mr Pilchard's friend asked if his boss was happy with his day's purchases and the dealer replied he thought they'd amassed a decent haul but there was one outstanding buy that really excited him. It turned out he considered ME the star bargain of the day, the jewel in the crown of fairground salvage! He thought I was an absolute 'one-off', a hybrid of old and new. "That horse is a winner. A Victorian rocking horse re-purposed as a carousel mount off a War-themed ride, in original used condition. You couldn't make it up!" he finished triumphantly. His friend retorted, "Just looks like an old nag with painted wings that got shot down in the war and crashed." Mr Pilchard roared with laughter at the comment and said pointedly, "That's why I'm the organ grinder and you're the monkey! He's more like the mythical Greek boy who flew too close to the sun and melted his wings. I'll call the little fellah 'Icarus' and I'll make sure he flies again. Hopefully, he'll fly out of my sale room for a massive profit!" The guffawing and ribbing continued for the entire journey. They could laugh and joke as much as they liked; the fact that I was a valued item and could turn them a profit meant I might find a lovely knowledgeable home. I happily imagined someone returning me to what I once was, a quality traditional rocking horse. My spirits lifted considerably as we bumped along the road towards my unknown future.

1957. My new temporary home was a clean and well-equipped workshop in a decent area of London, where I was treated with great care and respect. This made a lovely change and I admit I really enjoyed the pampering. However, I just couldn't understand why the man put in charge of me took such care retaining that tasteless paint all over my body. He carefully cleaned and tried to preserve all that awful faded, chipped and peeling decoration that Mauler's men had applied. The shabby white background colour that hid my wonderful dapples was delicately sponged and the gaudy tones of orange and red flames were lovingly brightened with a tiny brush dipped in some sort of spirit. He even gently washed what remained of my hacked mane and tail in soft baby shampoo. I'm very sad to say, none of Hovis' hair that had been woven through mine had lasted. That had long since fallen out, but the thought of it reminded me of the old days and happier times. It filled me with sorrow to think of all the friends I had lost. My big regret is that people and horses didn't seem to last as long as rocking horses. Again, I wondered, as I often had over the years, if my dearest friend Cobweb had survived and if so, what had become of him?

Before I was ready to hit the market, my 'renovator' did two dreadful things to me. He fitted a short metal fake roundabout pole into my pommel hole to represent me as a carousel horse but then attached me to a very ugly swing-stand, so I was also a rocking horse. The stand was lacking in any fine carving and with no turned pillars or chamfering, it just resembled two coarse lumpy posts joined with rails. Not at all what I had in mind, but I'd grown accustomed to others' ideas of beauty and as usual, had to swallow any vestige of pride I had left.

"Change is the law of life."

It wasn't long before I 'flew off the shelf' as predicted, for quite a large sum of money I might add, which made Mr Pilchard very pleased with himself as it vindicated him in the eyes of his sceptical partner. The dealer had advertised me as 'A rare, old and unusual carousel- style horse on a rocking stand that represents the mythical character Icarus'. He had ignored everything accurate he'd been told about my provenance by Nelson's grandfather and instead re-invented me as a weird hybrid. Apparently, ordinary rocking horses were two a penny compared to the valuable rarity that I had now become. After all, it was all about knowing your market to make a profit. The new buyer had asked that my worn red plastic saddle was replaced with a real leather one, which slightly galled Mr Pilchard as he thought the plastic one enhanced my 'retro' look. He had shrugged, saying the client had paid handsomely and he could always use the red one on another horse. After rummaging around in his stores, he found the remnants of a tatty light tan saddle with half the flaps missing. He had no qualms about nailing this to my back with old studs and even included some similar straps, which he placed on my head as a matching bridle. He was pleased with himself as it hadn't cost him a penny.

They loaded me with extra care and I was transported by van to my latest home, another on the long list of homes I'd experienced over the last fifty-seven years. I'd decided to stop guessing or worrying about what my future might hold. When you get to my age and look back, the world seems to have changed so fast. My head would spin if I tried to think too much, so I've learned to go along with the flow of things and try to accept change. Nothing stays the same, good or bad. Time rolls on relentlessly.

1967. As it turned out, my new home was perfectly pleasant, and I spent a contented ten years there. The family installed me into their large converted warehouse apartment which doubled as their studio. It was a trendy home, unlike any I'd seen before. Weird and wonderful artefacts and objets d'art from all over the globe decorated this airy flat. There was a huge open-plan area with a kitchen at one end and some low divan beds at the other. Giant cushions and bean bags were scattered around, giving a great atmosphere of relaxed comfort. A massive circular glass table made from an ancient cartwheel graced the centre of the space and seemed to be the hub of all activities. I was placed next to one of the many long factory-style crittall windows. The view from this high vantage point was spectacular, but life here was so hectic and interesting, I hardly had time for gazing. My family were artists: Anna worked with silver jewellery and Tarquin was a painter. Their children were twins with beautiful blonde hair and large green-grey eyes that reminded me of Diesel's. They were seven years old; the girl was called India and the boy had an unusual name that I loved, he had been named Javalindsey.

Indi and Jav, as they were referred to, were kind and polite but tended to run free and wild in their paradise home, thoroughly enjoying themselves by hurtling about on the beanbags or scribbling on large sheets of paper laid down on the floor for them, allowing them to be creative. There was no harsh discipline or routine, yet those children were lovely to live with, always being careful and respectful of the beautiful pieces of exotic art that could be found in every inch of the place. They were home-educated by their capable mother and took their lessons seriously. The instruction was on a wide variety of topics including art, and I learned so much, just listening. The children knew every detail of all the pieces and paintings in the flat, where they hailed from and what they represented. Both children loved to work alongside their parents; Indi would pick flowers from the nearby London park and make earrings or daisy chain necklaces mimicking her mother's jewellery, which she often placed around my neck. Jav was very keen on drawing and would sometimes sit near me with pencil and paper to do various sketches of me. I was flattered to be a model, even though I certainly didn't look how I would have wished.

Although I was happy enough, something in my life was missing. Like the Rectory, this home was full of love, laughter and delightful children, but I felt unfulfilled. Indi and Jav were not fussed about riding me; they rarely climbed aboard to have a ride, they were more interested in decorating me or dressing me up. Also, I noticed they never talked to me. Perhaps, being twins, they had each other for closeness and didn't need a strange looking horse as a confidante. I think I missed the special bond I'd experienced with other children. The most attention I received from little Jav was when he decided to paint me. Oh dear, I really didn't need more ghastly paint over my already hidden dapples, but Diesel's wise words rang in my ears. Don't be a snob, he'd said, the kiddies need their fun.

I'm not sure Mr Pilchard would've have approved, after the trouble he'd gone to in keeping my fairground décor intact. Luckily, the paint Jav applied to me in slavers of sloppy chalky white was a removable emulsion type. He had such fun with his task of painting me; imitating his father, he would step back to assess his work critically through screwed-up eyes and then step forward to complete the next area of my body. He took his time on my legs, swirling his brush round and round so as not to miss the undersides. When he'd splashed more paint industriously over my other side, he declared his work of art finished. I thought there would be trouble when his father saw what Jav had done to his very expensive 'hybrid horse' purchase, not to mention the state of the floor all around me. But I was wrong. The man praised his son warmly for doing a lovely job and said gently, "What do we artists do when we've finished our work?" Jav smiled and answered brightly, "Clean up!". The boy ran off excitedly to fetch a bucket and mop and he and his father had more fun cleaning up the mess.

It was a touching sight to see the love they shared. That was a real eye-opener for me and made me think how different life was for this little boy, compared to that of poor Augustus and the upbringing he had received at the hands of his brutal father. The world had changed and moved on so fast, it was hard to take in. Indi was given the same sort of love and encouragement from her mother, who complimented her efforts in bedecking me in various decorations. I'd never seen children brought up like this, with so much care lavished on them, yet with total freedom to do as they liked.

When Jav's handiwork on my body had dried, the twins collaborated to complete my 'look' by adding large colourful circular spots. Then India grabbed a felt pen and giggling with her brother, she wrote my newest name of 'Icarus' just below my left wing. She was so proud that she'd spelled it correctly and she and Jav danced round me singing a silly song about getting too near to the sun. I admit I did enjoy watching them play so happily. Their sheer delight working together in such harmony made it obvious to me that they had never really needed me. Perhaps that's why I felt lonely, even though I was surrounded by a warm family. Or perhaps I was just pining for my little rider Jaqueline. I had lost her forever. I still felt an ache in my heart every time I thought about her.

After ten interesting years with this family, I felt I had gained more knowledge of the world. It had been fascinating to observe the bustling London streets through the apartment window of my high seat. However, as always, it was time to move on. My family had decided to expand their children's education by taking them on extensive travels, exploring art in various countries of the East.

I was to be auctioned. I gathered this was a type of sale where people bid against each other to secure what they wanted. It was daunting yet quite exciting. I no longer feared what life had in store for me because worrying was a waste of energy as it could not change an outcome. I would worry if I felt my situation warranted it. Wise old Diesel's philosophy was rubbing off on me! There were no sad farewells or sentimental goodbyes given to me. Everyone was too pre-occupied with their impending adventure. After all, to them I had just been an interesting piece of art sculpture, nothing more. I was simply wrapped up with other valuable articles and shipped off to the sales room, soon to be starting a new life… with whom or where, I had no idea.

Chapter 13 'Lot 67'

"Perseverance takes perseverance."

1967

The auction was the setting of a strange and emotional day, but one of the happiest in my life! What happened at that auction house beggars belief, but I will try my best to describe what went on and how it all finished up.

There were three people in the room that day, all very keen to have me for their own. One of them was a quiet-spoken, tall, dark stranger who kept himself to himself. It was my dearest friend Manfri. I told you he never gave up searching for me. How he tracked me down was purely due to persistence, know-how and a bit of Romany luck. His nephew Roybin had been labouring on fairgrounds for a few years and had ended up working for Mauler and Sons. He'd heard through Nelson, my friend the fairground-boy and his old grandfather, about the beautiful little rocking horse that had been mistakenly used on a carousel ride years earlier. Roybin's ears had pricked up at this story as he knew all about my theft being connected to a funfair and the determination of his uncle to find me. Nelson gave him an old photo that he'd taken when his niece had ridden me one summer, to see if I might be recognised by his uncle. Roybin had excitedly given Manfri this information and the photo for my identity to be confirmed. His uncle had been delighted that the 'patrin' hadn't gone cold and that the hunt was still on. Of course, it was me, Bokki, in the photo! Manfri had said that despite the paint, there was no mistaking my fine head and beautiful big eye. Next, he'd asked his nephew to try and discover where I had gone. Roybin later passed on the name of the dealer who had bought me, a Mr Pilchard.

Manfri immediately caught a train to London, where he found the dealer's workshop and armed with the old photo of me on the roundabout, approached the man for information. At first Mr Pilchard was very wary and swore he'd bought me 'fair and square', but that had been over ten years ago. He wondered just how valuable I must have been to have someone so hot on my trail, and secretly wished he'd asked the artist for more money. Manfri crossed the dealer's palm with silver which revealed my last known address. Then the trail was nearly lost, because when Manfri arrived at the warehouse flat, new people had just moved in. They said the artist and his family had gone abroad…but that all their 'arty' things had gone to be auctioned.

If Manfri was good at one thing, it was 'calling' or knocking on people's doors, a remnant of his totting days. He didn't hesitate, but rang every doorbell in the street, enquiring if anybody had seen the name of a van that might have taken the artist's belongings to an auction house. Eventually, a lady remembered a sign-written van with the odd name 'One Man's Treasure' on the side. Manfri chuckled to himself as it reminded him of his dear Uncle Jed's old totting maxim, only then it had been 'One man's tat is our treasure!' It didn't take him long to trace the address of the sale room in question and he was told that the sale items were being viewed on the morrow, ready to be auctioned the following day.

Manfri came to see me before the big day. He chose his moment carefully when not a soul was about. I was literally shaking with joy and disbelief at hearing his voice and seeing him after so long. A grown man shedding a tear and kissing a shabby toy horse would have been a strange sight, so I'm glad we had that moment to ourselves. He whispered, "I'll try me best t'buy ya, Bokki, but I ain't got a lot'a vonga (money), only what I'se kept back from Airborne's big win. Wotever happens, I'll keep tabs on ya this time." Manfri had finally caught up with me…and just in time.

"We should not let our fears hold us back from pursuing our hopes." – **John F. Kennedy**

On the day of the sale, two young women were sat drinking mugs of coffee and talking earnestly at a table in the café opposite the auction house. They were poring over a catalogue, scrutinizing a well-creased page that had been thumbed through a hundred times in the past few days. The taller of the two said, "Are you positive you want that particular one? There are others in much better condition, proper rocking horses, you know, classical ones, like mine." The petite blonde woman studied the tiny printed image of the scruffy well-used horse that was Lot 67 and answered stubbornly, "No, it's him I want. Only him. He reminds me of that one I told you about. The one I rode when the fair came to town when we were kids." Her friend retorted that she could hardly forget, because the story of that horse – and the fanciful account of a midnight ride, had been repeated so many times during the past eleven years, it was beginning to wear thin. She continued, "But why THAT one, it doesn't even look like a fairground horse or whatever they've got it down as!" Her friend replied quietly, "Nor did he, but it looks just like him." The other woman sighed. "You've never been the same since I bought my one last year. You're obsessed – all over again. The quicker we buy you this fellow, the better!" she added resignedly. The smaller woman glanced at her watch and said, "Sorry for being such a bore, June, but I'm worried I won't be able to stretch too much above his reserve. Let's at least go and see what I'm about to spend my inheritance on. They should be letting us in to view about now."

There wasn't long to go before bidding started. A huge crowd was forming in the viewing areas; people were bustling about trying to get a final glimpse of their desired object, trying to decide on a ceiling price that they must not bid above. Auctions are funny places. Psychology plays a big part, often the price of something is driven up beyond the realms of good sense because a battle between two buyers ensues, neither wanting to admit defeat. This is often termed 'bidding fever' and June warned her friend against falling into this trap. Lot 67 was described simply as 'Icarus. A C20th wooden carousel horse on a stand' and was surrounded by interested individuals, some serious dealers, some just curious. It was nigh on impossible to get near.

Although flattering to have all this attention, it was very worrying. Four other old rocking horses stood near me, all quite lifeless and I'm sorry to say, not very inspiring. Despite their recently-applied shiny paintwork and thick, flowing hair, they seemed to have no soul. I felt they had been carved without care and lacked any flow or elegance. There must have been something interesting about me as I had attracted a crowd and I hoped that wouldn't cause my price to rise. I needed to be sold cheaply, so that Manfri could afford to buy me. Then I noticed two young women trying desperately to view me. They were pushing politely through the crowd, only to be engulfed by more bodies blocking their path, until a small gap appeared. That's when I saw her. That earnest, serious face looking longingly at me, of course – I'd seen that same look eleven years earlier. My heart thumped so loudly, I thought the woman standing by me would hear it. As our eyes met, we recognised each other simultaneously. It was Jacqueline, the love of my life, the little girl I'd missed so badly... and as her lips formed the word 'Zeppy', the sound was lost in the busy room.

The tannoy announced that bidding was about to commence and everyone rushed off to get their seats. In the confusion, I lost sight of Jacqueline as her friend dragged her by the arm in the direction of the others. Oh, I was in turmoil. Two people whom I really loved, were going to fight each other to buy me! Then there was that other kindly woman who had shown genuine interest. I sensed she really wanted me, a person I had instantly liked. I knew instinctively she was someone who understood who and what I was...

That rather nice woman, like Manfri, had come to view me the day before. In fact, they had passed like ships in the night. Manfri had waited in the shadows while a host of potential buyers had pored over me. They had inspected my three layers of paint, checked the solidity of my body and legs and even peered into my broken mouth and cracked jaw. This latest injury had occurred when I was transported to the auction storerooms, but by this stage of my life, I had gone beyond caring what I looked like. My vanity had now disappeared, which I think was a good thing and had helped me to survive.

As Manfri was about to approach and surprise me, he'd had to pull back into the corner again when he realised someone else had been playing his waiting game but had beaten him to it. This woman appeared from nowhere and took her opportunity when the others had moved on, striding purposefully towards me with an air of quiet confidence. She gazed at me for a full minute and sighed in appreciation of my beauty – well, I like to think it was that. Then she gently laid a hand on me, fingers tracing my deeply carved neck, over my proud chest down to my fine forelegs, appreciating my realistic form. She felt all my limbs as she might a real-life horse, curving her fingers round my pasterns. I'm sure she realised where I'd come from, as Nelson's grandfather had. Something about her calm appraisal made me think she had great knowledge. She'd recognised my quality and knew then, she must buy me. Romany folk are astute judges of character and after watching this woman inspect me, Manfri couldn't help himself warm towards her. He knew instinctively she was a genuine person but he also feared she'd be his most dangerous adversary in the auction. But he hadn't reckoned on Jacqueline and June.

When Lot 66 had been sold, they brought me in and placed me in front of the auctioneer. I felt as if I was on trial and sick with anticipation. Perhaps now, I thought, may be the time to worry.

The bidding was lively at first but tailed off as the bargain-hunters dropped out, realising there were three very determined people in the crowd. One was bidding for an old and loved friend, the other for her childhood dream and the third, a rocking horse restorer, was bidding for my quality and because she wanted to return me to my former glory. All three had good reason to buy me, but it was going to be down to finance in the end. If only they had met beforehand and worked something out between them…

Jacqueline fell first. She had bid with a loud and fierce determination, hoping to scare off any opposition. When the price had gone up beyond her means, to June's horror, she had unwisely kept going. Her friend hissed at her to stop and grabbed hold of her arm to prevent any further bidding. She'd shrugged her friend off angrily saying, "But it's actually HIM. I recognised him when we got closer. It's Zeppy from that fairground, you can't possibly understand how terrible this is, to lose him now…" Her anguished cry of disappointment when she knew she'd lost me was heart-wrenching for the both of us and didn't go un-noticed by the last two bidders in the battle.

Manfri was craftier with his bidding and a discreet wink to the auctioneer had my price rise several times after Jacqueline was forced to drop out. His opponent had located the desperate young woman who had gone against her, but she'd failed to spot this persistent yet invisible bidder she was now battling. Manfri, however, too shrewd to be a victim of 'bidding fever', stopped as soon as his ceiling price was reached. He melted away silently and his identity remained a mystery to the woman who eventually won her prize. As no more bids were forthcoming, the auctioneer declared "Fair warning…SOLD" The gavel slammed down, and with it, all my hopes of being re-united with either of my beloved friends. This was one of the lowest points of my life. The rollercoaster of emotions I'd felt over the last two days had flat-lined.

Well, you know me by now and you know that when I'm down, I pick myself up and hope for something better to happen. And it certainly did! I should have known I'd see Manfri again because he'd promised to keep 'tabs' on me so he'd always know where I was. Strangely, I couldn't see him when I was carried out to the storeroom after the sale. My lovely Jacqueline was there, though, waiting to greet me with both joy and sadness. We both felt so good to be close to one another again. She stood possessively by my side and I could feel her hand trembling on my neck as my new owner approached after she'd completed the sales paperwork. She was faced with the two young women she'd seen bidding against her. "What do you want him for?" Jacqueline demanded in an emotional, slightly hostile voice. My new woman could clearly read the acute disappointment and sadness showing on a face which she recognised could have been her own, when she had lost out on a much-desired object. I had felt her empathy and it drew me closer to her. She knew she must be kind, so calmly and gently introduced herself as Brenda.

June decided civility was the best way forward and did the same, introducing herself and her friend as June and Jacs. "They call us the two Js and we've been friends since we were tiny. Sorry about Jacs. She's just so disappointed to have missed out. She's been trying to buy a horse like him since she rode one at a fairground eleven years ago and then she realised that this horse actually IS him, the very horse she rode. It's so sad she's lost him now because she's dreamed about him all these years… And frankly, it's making my life unbearable, especially since I bought myself one last year…" After this rather rambling explanation, June felt rather embarrassed but it was met with a warm, understanding smile from Brenda. "I see," she replied quietly. "Well, if you wait until these men wrap him up for me, we can take him and ourselves off to the café and have a good chat over a cup of tea. I'll explain who I am and why I've bought him."

"The first duty of love is to listen." – **Paul Tillich**

Why I presumed Manfri wasn't present, I can't imagine, for I knew him better than that, he was a man of shadows. Of course he was there, listening to every word. In his game, forewarned was forearmed and you played your cards close to your chest. He was assessing everyone carefully before showing them his hand… So, when the four of us met in the café, there was another man sitting quietly nearby, biding his time. Brenda had me by her side, all wrapped up, able to see a bit but hear everything. Opposite sat the two Js, June excited to hear what the woman had to say and Jacs, in a slightly calmer and more forgiving mood. Once they had their cups of tea in front of them, Brenda explained that her job was to restore rocking horses and bring them back to their former selves. She felt I was especially lovely and deserved her attention. Continuing steadily, she concluded that I was in need of a lot of work to preserve me for future generations. Then she warned that many beautiful horses had been allowed to fall into a state of disrepair or worse, to a point beyond help. In her opinion, I needed rescuing, but it would take a lot of effort, skill and expense to return me to how I would have been originally.

This speech hit home with all who were listening and June was the first to break the sombre silence. "Yes, I think you are the best person to have bought him. Don't you agree, Jacs?"

My clever little Jacqueline's mind had been racing and she'd hatched a plan. She spoke clearly and with deliberation. "I suppose you are, but once he's mended, what will you do with him? Do you keep all the ones you've rescued?"

Brenda laughed kindly at the idea and replied wistfully, "Oh, if only I could! But no, I then have to find them a good home, but obviously I must make a profit or I couldn't eat!"

"Well," Jacs said tentatively, "what if I buy him off you after you've restored him?"

Another awkward silence ensued which was broken once again by June. "Don't be silly, Jacs. You heard Brenda, it'll cost loads to do him up and you couldn't even afford him in the state he's in today."

My heart was sinking fast, I willed Manfri to come to the rescue, which he did, right on cue!

A man rose from the table next to theirs and strode towards the seated women. "Scuse me, ladies, but I needs ta talk ta youz about th' liddle hoss!" He then slapped a tattered bulging brown envelope in the middle of their table. To say they were surprised would be an understatement. The sudden arrival of this tall, weather-beaten stranger had shocked them. With his piercing yet twinkling black-brown eyes, ruddy complexion and mop of iron grey hair, he cut a rather handsome figure.

Brenda straight away said triumphantly, "The mysterious 'other' bidder!"

Jacs frowned, looked him up and down, then said in a hesitant whisper, "You do look familiar, are you Manfri and do you have a sister called Sinni?"

For once in his life, he was taken aback and racked his brains, trying to recognise her. But he couldn't and had no idea how she could know such a thing. She, of course, had paid a fleeting visit to this brother and sister eleven years earlier, during that marvellous tour I gave her of my life!

June looked blankly at the others and said flatly, "I have absolutely no idea what's going on…"

Looking up at Manfri, Brenda touched the envelope and asked what it was for. He instructed her to open it. The very substantial amount of money inside was another shock. Then he reassured everyone that the money had been won legitimately years ago and had been sitting safely in a bank. He had drawn it out specifically to buy me back but had lost the bid. All he asked now was that when Brenda had finished working on me, that she should let Jacs buy me with the help of his savings. He added, "It's only right. A blind man c'n see she loves th' liddle hoss."

Brenda was really puzzled by this man's generous offer. She asked

Manfri if he'd met the two friends before or if I had ever been his horse. Looking over to me and smiling, he told her he'd never met anyone before, but yes, he'd known me almost all his life since meeting me in an orphanage. He explained how he and his sister had then rescued me from a bonfire and how later, their teacher had recognised me as her brother's childhood nursery rocking horse. He ended by saying he had kept in touch with me all through my life until the day I was stolen for the fair. He added softly, it was important that he always knew where I was. There were a lot of people who loved me dearly and would be so happy to know he'd found me. He then pushed the envelope towards Brenda, saying, "This is money t'keep him safe."

Brenda needed more time before making any decisions and slid the money back to the centre of the table. All this information had surprised and pleased her as knowledge of a horse you are about to restore can be so fascinating. She invited Manfri to draw another chair up to the table. Needing to know more about the young woman's involvement in all this, she turned to Jacs and asked her how long she had known me. In a rather shy voice, she answered, "I've only known him for one night but it felt like a lifetime, I can't tell you why, you'll think me crazy…" Manfri encouraged her to tell her story, saying the two of them knew, but everyone else deserved to know just how special I was. So the tale of the midnight ride was started. "Well, in those days, he didn't look anything like now. He was painted all bright colours and had massive wings and his golden pole… but I could always recognise him by that beautiful little head and his eyes. He's got life in him, you know that, don't you?" She looked round at each person's face expectantly, seeing only Manfri's reassuring nod and wink, which gave her the courage to continue. She explained about the themed War Horse ride and all the named horses. She'd picked me out because she had felt this amazing surge of love and had been drawn to me by an unseen force. Jacs was almost back in her dream as she re-lived the feeling of that first ride. It was like she'd made a life-long friend and we had somehow connected forever. Then she told her audience about returning later that night, our crazy spinning journey that ensued and the experience of me taking her back through my life. The part of the tale when she'd returned to the fairground to find me gone and the misery and heartbreak she'd felt for years after, was really hard for me to hear. She ended, "I know it sounds absolutely crackers, but it seemed so real. And he trusted me enough to show me a glimpse of his past. That means a lot." She hung her head, suddenly exhausted by the emotional toll of telling her story and the fear of losing me again.

Then June admitted that she'd never believed any of it had happened, but thought her friend had just had a vivid dream. "But now... I really don't know what to think." Manfri then pointed out that Jacs had recognised him. How could she have possibly known him and his sister's name, if her story was just a dream? There was a hush around the table; it was a lot to digest. All eyes turned to stare at me but I stood there, all wrapped up, looking quite innocent. Brenda then said very sensibly, "Well, there you are. There are some things that just can't be explained. We'll leave it at that." At that moment, I felt so happy, like I was grinning inside! I DID notice a distinct wink from Manfri! For the first time in ages, I felt complete again.

Before our strange but enlightening meeting around that café table was over, new friendships had been made. It was decided that everyone would meet up at Brenda's farm in Dorset to visit me periodically, as I was being restored. At the end of the process, Jacs and Manfri would pool their money together to purchase me from Brenda. They would own me jointly, but Jacs was to be my keeper and I would be in her care. Manfri explained that he was constantly on the move and it would be impossible for him to take me. All he needed out of the deal was to know I was safe. Nothing was put in writing except an exchange of contact details. They all trusted one another. My welfare had been the catalyst that joined them together. Manfri carried me to Brenda's vehicle and once I was safely loaded, he made everyone spit on their palms and slap hands, the traditional way of cementing an unbreakable deal. With the promise secured, he said his final words to the women, spoken with genuine warmth: "I'm really pleased I met youz three today. Thank you for rokkering (talking) to me, an' kushti bok to youz!" I understood perfectly but they looked quite baffled at the unfamiliar Romany words! He then slipped away silently, leaving each of the women feeling strangely charmed and uplifted as they made their way home.

CHAPTER 14. B.L.I.T.Z.

"Destiny is the vision to realise your dreams and perseverance to work towards them."

1970

It has been three years since that auction day and my life is so blissful now, I can't tell you! Sometimes I'm a little scared something will happen to spoil my joy, as I've learned from past experiences to never take anything for granted… However, now I am surrounded by people who treasure me, and whatever happens in the future, I'm confident someone will always be there to offer their help. Actually, I've rarely felt so safe. When you reach the grand old age of seventy, you need some security and I have that now. Also, I've been made to feel young and healthy, like a cheeky colt again. I am as strong now, as I was when Wilf, my Maker, sent me off into the world all those years ago.

Let me explain about this momentous change. Essentially, I've been re-born! Although I've been 'restored' to my former glory, there is an important difference. My new friend Brenda turned out to be as wonderful as we all thought from our first meeting in that cafe. She is a fine artist and during the process, she did not rub out my past. I am still very much ME. I have my original features back and I have retained my integrity and age. Not like those rocking horses that were with me at the auction, those poor lifeless souls had been made to look brand new with no character or history left in them. I still have my 'wear and tear', every little nick, dent and worn patch showing on my body to remind me of my fantastic and eventful former life. I still look every inch my age in a distinguished sort of way, but I have been made strong and sound. Admittedly, I do now have a beautiful new harness and real flowing horse-hair again. The dress-rehearsal for that was quite a hoot, but I'll tell you about that later. Now it's time to go back in my story and explain what befell me and my friends after that amazing day of the sale back in 1967.

Everyone had returned home from London in a state of dazed wonderment. Manfri could not believe his incredible good luck that had led to him finding me. Although the outcome was one he'd never imagined, he was very satisfied. Now it was someone else's turn to enjoy me and have the pleasure of my company. As long as the people to whom I was important knew I was safe, he felt it was only right I should go to someone like Jacs who obviously adored me. During his long train journey home to the New Forest, Manfri had an interesting thought and the seed of an idea was planted. As he reminisced about the times we'd spent together over the years, he realised that every detail his memory could afford him had always been carefully stored within his head as vivid pictures. Grace had always said he and Sinni had good retentive memories.

Now, he would do the remembering and maybe someone who felt his same passion, could take his pictures and turn them into words. He decided then and there that all the people who had shared their life with me should record their memories. This idea grew into a conviction that between them, they should attempt to write my story.

As soon as Manfri returned home from London, the news of his success spread like wildfire. He telephoned Grace in Epsom and told her the outcome of his quest. He explained about the deal he had struck with three amazing strangers, who could now be considered friends. Grace, now in her seventies, was overcome with joy and relief. Her daughter Izzy was also overwhelmed. All the family were excited and grateful to know I was safe, despite the strange life I'd apparently led since being stolen. They all wanted to see me as soon as possible. Sinni was delighted I'd been found and said it reminded her of the incredulous joy she'd felt when she'd discovered me on the bonfire heap. Roybin swelled with pride at his part in finding me, and all Manfri's family celebrated the event with a huge party and much feasting, singing and dancing. I had become a bit of a legend among the Forest's Romany folk! Roybin, now back home from the fair, wrote to his friend Nelson and his grandfather to let them know I'd been found and to thank them for their invaluable help. A trip for everyone to visit me at Brenda's farm in Dorset was planned for the future. Grace and Izzy also wished to meet Jacs and June, who were going to play an important role in my future. As you can imagine, Manfri's idea of writing my 'memoirs' was received with great enthusiasm by Grace. After all, she had been his beloved teacher many years earlier. They decided to broach the subject with the others when they eventually met and got to know them.

The two Js had driven home in a numbed silence. It had been an emotional day. Initially Jacs had felt perfectly resigned to the recent agreement, but after a while she'd slumped into a depression. Always straight-talking and to the point, June declared that today, she thought the perfect outcome had been reached and inquired why her friend was so glum. Jacs had answered sulkily that the best outcome would have been if I was coming home with them right now, not being shipped off to some farm miles away with Brenda. June lost patience and retorted harshly, "Oh, I despair! I can't believe your attitude. You've spent your adult life chasing your childhood dream and now it's about to happen, you're still not happy! That man is kind enough to share his horse with you and you've been promised he'll be done up and then you'll have him at home…and you're still moaning? I can't believe you!" After a thoughtful silence, Jacs apologised and agreed it made good sense for me to be restored correctly. She admitted she trusted both Brenda and Manfri, and, on reflection, was very grateful for the way things had turned out. They decided the process of my restoration could be quite exciting and who knew what adventures lay ahead. The rest of the journey home was spent happily planning future trips to Dorset.

It would have been a long and tedious drive home for Brenda. She was used to trawling all over the country searching for quality rocking horses to 'rescue'. Somehow this journey was different. The hours flew past unnoticed as she tried to make sense of the strange events of that afternoon. Her thoughts were jumbled up and needed to be put in order. Firstly, she had secured one of the loveliest horses she'd seen in a long time; she was sure I was from the Paul Leach workshop. Being a successful bidder was always a thrill, but this win had at first been marred by the desolation of a young woman who had tried desperately to obtain her childhood dream. Then she thought about the mysterious, charismatic stranger who had appeared in the café. His extraordinary offer to help Jacs to buy the horse back was quite inexplicable, yet she felt it was genuine. Of course, she couldn't forget that rather magical tale of the midnight ride and, to be honest, an explanation evaded her. Somehow it didn't seem that important, certainly nothing to worry about.

It was true that a few horses she'd worked on in the past seemed to possess a spirit and character of their own that would develop as she brought them back to health. It was all a part of truly loving your work as a restorer and making a difference to them. Nothing that spooked her, just a bit of anthropomorphism, perhaps… In the end, her conclusion of the day was simple; both Manfri and Jacs had loved me dearly and their knowledge held a key to my past. It was intriguing to know the history of a horse you were to work on. The information could make restoration so interesting, and it filled her with excitement. She would honour the deal and let them have first refusal to buy me when she'd finished. Nothing was more rewarding than sending a horse off to an appreciative home. One thing she was convinced of: I was a very special rocking horse. Brenda had now reached the county of Dorset and was only about twenty minutes away from her farm. Casually glancing over her shoulder, she said, "Not long now, lad. Nearly home." And then grinned as she realised she was already conversing with her new project.

"A time for the heart to heal, the body to mend and the soul to sing."

As I was off-loaded from Brenda's vehicle, the first thing that hit me was the wonderful scent of fresh evening air, still carrying hints of ripening wheat and newly rained-upon ground. It was a far cry from all my years in London with its smog and fumes. I welcomed the fact that now I was to live in the deep Dorset countryside. It brought back memories of my time in that glorious village of Hidley, surrounded by fields, woods and the nearby chalk grasslands of the North Downs.

I was taken to Brenda's workshop and gently unwrapped. There I stood in all my hybrid glory, feeling somewhat embarrassed. All around me was a selection of rocking horse faces looking curiously at me, all in various stages of repair. I could sense that some of these characters were like me and I knew we would be conversing together soon enough. I did glance round in a forlorn hope of seeing my long-lost friend Cobweb, but his exquisite, sweet face with his slightly large ears that I'd always teased him about, was nowhere to be seen. Oh, how I missed that wise little fellow. How many tales we could we have told each other. Mind you, the way I looked at present may have taken some explaining and I'm sure he would have got his own back, teasing me.

Very soon, my transformation began. The first job was to remove all those layers of paint. The fake funfair pole had been discarded at the sales to enable me to fit in my new owner's vehicle. Over the next week, Brenda had talked to Grace, Manfri and Jacs on the telephone to ask them how they remembered me. Grace had been too young to recall exactly how I looked when I'd first arrived at Kilwick, but said Gus had always boasted that I'd been the most splendid and costly horse in the shop. Jacs had described my fairground 'look' of orange and red flames on a white body, large wings painted on my flanks and the name 'Zepp-something' on my neck. The gaudy crimson parts of my face and the exaggerated black eyelashes were still visible, as Javalindsey had omitted touching my head when he and his sister had overpainted me in white and added those huge colourful spots. Manfri's take on my former appearance was more poetic. He simply said, "He were the colour of a thundery sky, covered from head t' foot in a hundred liddle moons."

1968. Over the next few months Brenda kept in touch with everyone, giving them progress reports. It was decided that no-one should see me until she was three-quarters of the way through her work. I had suffered physical abuse during the tough years but nothing that was life-threatening. My true identity had been somewhat lost along the way. I needed Brenda's restoration skills and she needed me to shine through by myself. It was just me and her now.

Javalindsey's emulsion handiwork came off easily. That awful, coarse black eye make-up became a distant memory as my old Victorian spidery lashes were carefully revealed and re-instated. Now, Brenda's biggest challenge was to remove the old white gloss from my body without damaging any signs of delicate paint underneath. She fervently hoped she may reveal those authentic 'little moons', the dapples that Florence had skilfully decorated me with nearly seventy years earlier. My true colours, remembered by Grace, Manfri and Izzy were just waiting to emerge.

Brenda and I became close during that tense process; with every painstaking chip and flake she removed, we celebrated silently as one by one, my beautiful dapples began to show. Oh, how I revelled in the care she took! Strangely enough the layers of fairground paint may have helped preserve me whilst I had been on the roundabout working in all weathers. She'd discovered the time-worn remnants of the name 'Zeppelin' ornately scrolled across my neck. She'd also spotted the faint lettering 'Icarus' that had been applied by little India in felt pen under one of my faded 'wax' wings. Every mark told a story and revealed a layer of my past.

Before I knew it, my body was nearly finished. The broken jaw and chipped ear had been flawlessly repaired. I had been strengthened, areas of chipped gesso repaired, paintwork stabilised, and body and limbs given a clean bill of health. My heart and spirits were sky-high as I had my dapples back again. I'd thoroughly enjoyed the whole restoration process; every day had brought me nearer to my old self.

In the spring, soon after I'd reached a 'three-quarter completed' stage, that long awaited day arrived when I was visited by my beloved friends. All through the process, Brenda had taken many photographs for everyone to be able to keep abreast of the progress made at each stage. They had seen my repairs and all the old paint coming off, but Brenda had left my beautiful re-instated dappled body as a surprise for them. The two Js drove into the farmyard first and Jacs rushed into the workshop to greet me. I must have looked very different as she literally gasped with delight. Before June and Brenda followed her in, she whispered, "You now look as beautiful on the outside as you are on the inside. I can't love you anymore than I do and soon I'll be seeing you every day." Then June saw me and exclaimed, "Wow, and wow! Now that's more like it! He's beginning to look like my fellow at home. He's turned out to be a proper rocking horse. Ooh, look at those old dapples, so like my one, they're really similar in many ways!"

*My heart and spirits were sky high as
I had my dapples back again.*

Next to arrive were Manfri, Grace, Izzy and her dear childhood friend, Ethel. Izzy had driven down with her mother and Ethel to meet Manfri near the New Forest. They had continued the journey with him to enable them to chat together. Half the trip had been spent discussing Manfri's idea of writing something down to document my life through everyone's memories. They had all agreed it was a lovely idea, but would take a lot of work and communication amongst themselves.

Brenda walked over to greet her next visitors, and everyone was introduced again before they all came into the workshop to see me. For Izzy and Grace, after many years thinking I was lost forever, it was an emotional meeting. Jacs drew back, suddenly feeling very shy and aware that I and these people shared a long and very strong connection. I think she felt guilty that she would be claiming me for herself. Oh, I wished I could tell her it was HER I wanted to go home with. The others had had their time with me. I would always love them dearly but now, Jacqueline and I needed the life together that we had been robbed of years ago. She watched with mixed feelings as I was joyfully re-united with wonderful Grace and my sweet Izzy. As they hugged me and kissed my face, I swayed dizzily under their embrace as I was not on a stand but just balancing on tip toes. Manfri stood a distance away, hands in pockets with a fond smile spread across his face. Whilst the others were talking excitedly about my wonderful transformation, he approached me and, peering appreciatively at me, whispered, "She's worked her magic on ya, Bokki. Yers as good as new but still the liddle hoss I's always known." Then he winked at me and chuckled, "Ya just can't take yer eyes off th' liddle blonde 'un, can ya!" Oh, Manfri knew me so well and what was in my heart. That was one day when I was grateful to have a heart! It wasn't bursting at all; my heart had more than enough room in it to love all those wonderful people whom I was lucky to have in my life.

Over the next few weeks there were more visits to the farm. Manfri often made the journey down but Grace could only come occasionally. Izzy, Ethel and her eldest son Eddie were always delighted to visit and see my progress week by week. The two Js and Eddie got on so well and had become good friends. The lad remembered riding me when he was a youngster at Jack Killadee's house by the yard. He and Izzy's daughter Mirabel used to spend hours riding me in turn, pretending to be famous jockeys. Those were the happy years before I had been mercilessly taken by thieves. Eddie told Jacs the legendary tale of Airborne's great win, a bedtime story that as a child he'd begged his mother to tell him many times. Funnily enough, both he and Jacs were born in the year 1946 and he had grown up dreaming that one day he would ride in the Derby. He even credited me for firing his racehorse passion! Eddie had taken after his grandfather Bert Yates, who had worked in the racing industry all his life and had taught Izzy and Ethel to ride. At 24, young Eddie Marland was proving a successful jockey who also worked in Epsom.

On one particular visit when Grace had been able to come, everyone had sat round Brenda's large farmhouse table and had spilled out their stories and memories. I was now installed in the kitchen and as they talked about my previous life, I listened and relived every moment. Brenda then announced she had a surprise up her sleeve. The time had come for me to have a new mane and tail attached. I was extremely excited because I'd felt rather naked all these years without my 'crowning glory' and was keen to feel some hair swinging about again. Several sets of horse-hair in a variety of colours were brought into the kitchen and Brenda told everyone they must help choose one that suited me.

I became a rather reluctant model, but I didn't mind as it was a pleasure to see everyone enjoying themselves so much. What a hilarious afternoon it turned out to be. My dear friends were falling about laughing as Brenda draped my head and neck in several hair swatches that somehow just didn't suit me. I remember one, which was actually made from a cow's tail. This had been a popular choice in the olden days when I was young. It was quite blonde and wavy and as it was lifted to my neck, my friends burst into fits of giggles. Jacs declared it made me look like Shirley Temple, whoever she was. Another very dark and straight swatch apparently gave me the look of Morticia of the Addams Family. Again, I had no idea what was causing everybody to laugh so much but I enjoyed being the centre of all the mirth. At last, after they had rejected one that made me resemble the Wild Man of Borneo (I have no clue who he is either, but I'm sure Diesel would have known all these characters), they all hit on one that was a resounding success. Grace and Manfri looked at each other and instantly said with quiet authority, "THAT'S the one." Well, I totally agreed, it was my favourite too and do you know why? It resembled the hair that Sinni had 'borrowed' from Hovis' mane many years ago, to weave through mine. It was exactly the right admixture of colours, dark and light greys and silvers with a slight hint of chestnut. It was perfect. Of course, this set in motion another story about my past, as often happened at the meetings around Brenda's table.

"What's in a name?" – **William Shakespeare**
"There is all the poetry in the world in a name."
– **Henry David Thoreau**

At one of our last ever get-togethers in Dorset, when Izzy had managed to bring Grace along to sit with us in Brenda's kitchen, an interesting conversation emerged. I was all but completed, with the most stunning tack now in place. Brenda had done me proud, making me an authentic saddle complete with a side-saddle pommel and child-sized antique stirrup irons, a fringed saddle cloth and a bridle of the very sort I would have worn when I was first sent out of the shop. I even had my silk rosettes back and wore a Victorian style bit in my mouth. Everyone was gazing at me in awe as I certainly was a sight to behold. All that was left was to place me securely on my beautiful hand-made stand and then I would be ready to go and live with Jacs.

Brenda started the conversation by asking what name they all called me. She added, "I was referring to him as the little Leach horse but you've obviously got your own names for him." Everyone spoke at once and a jumble of words spilled out, which made Brenda smile. Grace started off saying I was originally called Blizzard, but she was never keen on the name as it reminded her of her mean-spirited brother. Izzy continued, saying she and her mother always called me Lucky but when I was with Jack in the racing yard, I was known as Tinash. Manfri chipped in with his comment that Lucky was the translation of the Romany word Bokki. He and Sinni had always called me that since finding me on the bonfire, though at the orphanage I'd been called Sonny. Jacs added that she'd only ever known me as Zeppy because she'd only been able to read half of the word Zeppelin painted on my neck. Brenda reminded them that at the auction, I'd been advertised as Icarus and she'd subsequently discovered that name written in a child's hand under my painted left wing. My restorer then made an announcement. "I'm sure he's had other names but I think they probably belong in his past. But now...I have a surprise for you all."

The table was cleared and a space made in the centre. Brenda fetched a brown paper bag and put it down in front of a puzzled audience. "Look what I found inside your little horse when I had him on the bench!" she declared proudly. She gently tipped the contents out and an odd assortment of objects lay in front of everyone.

Grace reacted first; she gasped saying, "Oh Goodness, I'd forgotten all about his secret pommel hole!" Manfri and Izzy smiled at each other knowingly, but the others seemed baffled. Ethel, Eddie and the two Js were intrigued when Grace explained that when I first came to Kilwick, I'd originally had two side-saddle pommels, for the purpose of teaching little girls how to ride side-saddle. Gus had removed them, revealing the secret holes into my hollow belly. Some horses had one, some two. These orifices, hidden under most saddle flaps, were traditionally where generations of children had deposited various secret objects and treasures into rocking horses. June was excited and wondered if her horse at home had something similar and she couldn't wait to get back to investigate. She presumed older horses would possess them but newer ones may not, as side-saddle riding had fallen from favour in modern times. Ethel and Eddie declared they'd had no idea of its existence;

they'd seen a hole there as I was being restored but presumed it had been made for me to be fitted to the roundabout. Jacs was amazed that a secret place had been there all along. She'd had no clue because when she had ridden me, it had been hidden by my fairground pole and red plastic saddle.

Grace was the first to claim the objects she knew personally. She picked up the old splintered piece of my ear and the knob broken off the chest of drawers from her childhood nursery. As she clutched the items in her hand, she retold the tale of the rocking horse race that had ended in an accident and how Gus had hidden the evidence. She never mentioned the name of her little horse; I think the memory of losing him still caused her pain. Cobweb had been her only friend in a loveless house with a stern father and cruel brother. He'd been her only good memory of a lonely childhood. She laughed hollowly, remembering how terrified she'd been at the time.

Next, Manfri slid two items towards him; the rather frayed and disintegrating twig plus the small flower-head he'd carved for me. Secrets were his stock-in-trade and he'd known about my hidden 'keepsake' hole since first meeting me at the orphanage. Almost whispering to himself he said, "Tis a safe place for secrets…" He didn't go into detail but continued thoughtfully, "Them two things helped us find him and, I hope, fetched him a bit o luck." He advised it was a long story to be told another day.

Izzy then tentatively touched the rolled-up newspaper cuttings that she had posted into my belly during the height of the Second World War. The elastic band she'd used all those years ago had perished but the articles reporting the dreadful news of the day during war-time Britain had remained intact. Brenda had read them when she'd discovered everything inside me; it was a great bit of history relating to those times, but their contents had been sombre reading. Slowly and carefully, Izzy flattened them out, but said she'd rather not be reminded of the awful worry she'd felt for her family, trapped in London in the midst of continual bombings. Grace took her daughter's hand and gave it a gentle squeeze.

The other bits and pieces, a nail, boiled sweets and a pencil were of little consequence and were about to be discarded. Just as Brenda was sweeping them off the table with a cupped hand, Izzy suddenly exclaimed, "Hold on a minute! Whatever is that stuck to the sweet?" Around a dried-out piece of barley sugar was a piece of paper that everyone had dismissed as a scrap of old wrapper, but Izzy thought it was too thick and somehow looked familiar. It was the colour of the old-fashioned betting slip receipts she'd seen hundreds of times at Jack Killadee's house. She retrieved it from Brenda's hand, eased it off the sweet and very carefully opened the tightly folded slip. With a gasp of shock, Izzy read the faded type-written receipt. It showed an absolutely huge amount of stake money that had been wagered and the resulting thousands of pounds that had been won on horse No13 in a race dated 6.6.1946. That was the day of Airborne's Derby. Her mind went back to that plan she and Alec had hatched to try and win money enough to secure their future together. She remembered Alec's determination to place a wager despite Airborne's number. He'd declared "Number thirteen, lucky for some!" but Izzy had cautioned him not to risk everything he had. She knew the only person who could have hidden the slip inside me was Alec. Open-mouthed, she glared at Manfri who wore a bemused, apologetic grin. "You knew!" she blurted out accusingly. Chuckling, he said,

"Well, he couldn't tell ya the amount he wagered that day, ya never would'a let him put everything he owned in the world on a horse! But good come of it... he proposed to ya the very next day!" Well, I certainly had been a safe place for secrets...until I'd been tipped upside down!

Anyway, it was decided that the things that held precious memories were to be returned to my belly. I was most happy about that as, after all, those keepsakes were mine and I'd looked after them for everybody over many years. Eddie, ever the joker, remarked he was surprised I hadn't been struck down with a bout of colic, with all those bits rattling about in my belly!

Brenda then continued, "Anyway, my next bit of news is... I've come up with a new name for him. I've started calling him this since I found out his history and, well, I think it really suits him." Everyone looked at her expectantly. In a proud voice she announced her newly thought-up name. "BLITZ! I now call him Blitz." After being met with total silence Brenda continued quickly. "He really looked like he'd been through the wars, as they say, TWO wars actually and it ties him up with Izzy's cuttings and links him to his time at the fair on the War Horses ride and his Zeppelin character..." She trailed off disappointedly, fearing no-one thought it was an appropriate sort of name for a rocking horse.

Suddenly June broke the silence exclaiming, "Well, I think it's perfect, quite masterful. So original and snappy! I love it." Everybody was warming to the idea of a new name for a re-born horse, a name that could be universally used by all concerned. However, as Jacs was to have me full-time, everyone agreed it should be her decision what I should be called. My bright and imaginative Jacs had been very quiet up to that point, thinking and working things out in her head. All eyes turned to her as she cleared her throat and started spelling the name out. "B.L.I.T.Z. ... Do you realise that those are the initials of all the names that we've known him as? B for Bokki, L for Lucky, I for Icarus, T for Tinash and Z for Zeppi. Yes, it is perfect, a mix of all the names he's been loved with. Blitz it is then!" Well, they all clapped, Brenda opened a bottle of home-made mead and everyone drank a toast to me and my new name. I felt as if we were celebrating my birthday. That happy afternoon was the last time I saw my friends all together in Dorset; I was soon to be moving on again, but this time I felt my future was safe.

1968. So I went to live with the two Js. When her mother had died the previous year, Jacs had sold their house in Middlesex. She'd moved in with June to help her with her new business at her stud on the family's estate in Surrey, not too far from Epsom. Since moving nearer to Eddie, the two saw a lot of each other. June sensed a romance brewing which delighted her as she thought they were perfectly suited. My grand collection date was set for the 6th of June and Eddie offered to transport me back to Surrey in his van so he and the two Js picked Manfri up on the way down to Dorset. The four arrived to be greeted by a lovely lunch Brenda had prepared for them, before getting down to business. I was wrapped in plastic and ready to go. That deal made in the café was honoured. Jacs and Manfri pooled their resources and purchased me from my restorer. After farewells and promises to keep in touch, they drove away, dropping Manfri back to the New Forest before continuing for home. Home with Jacs, my long-held dream had come true. How ecstatic I'd felt during that drive, but I was unaware of a huge shock that was awaiting me just round the corner, another unexpected corner in my surprising life.

I've said it before and I'll say it again. Fact is stranger than fiction and I often feel a thread of magic has been woven through my whole life.

After the long journey back to Surrey, I was carefully lifted out of the van and brought into June's stylish art nouveau sitting room. Through the plastic wrapping, my eyes were drawn to the bright light pouring in from large French windows. Here I spotted the blurred silhouette of a rocking horse framed by those sun-lit panes. Not just any horse but an extremely elegant one with a lovely stretch to its limbs and a delicately sculpted head and curve of neck. Even with impaired vision I could tell this horse, mounted on sweeping bows, was one of great quality. It had unmistakable poise and charm that seemed eerily familiar…then it struck me – I recognised him! Oh, was it possible the horse in front of me might really be him? Could June's 'little fellow', the horse she'd constantly talked about, be my nursery pal Cobweb?

"Quick, let's unwrap him. He seems to be vibrating, it's like he's trembling!" Jacs muttered in a concerned voice. They decided to place me right next to my dearest friend whom I'd missed so much over the years. As we stood together, delighted to be re-united and drinking in each other's company, June introduced us. "There you are, Blitz, meet my chap Cobweb, a little friend for you. And welcome home!" Oh, if only they knew how welcomed I felt at that moment. My perceptive Jacs almost realised, as she could read me like a book. She remarked to June and Eddie that I'd calmed down now and it looked like the two of us just belonged together. "You'd think they were old dear friends, like you and me, June!" Out of the mouths of babes…

The next two years at June's house were full of happiness. Cobweb and I would stand shoulder to shoulder as we used to at Kilwick Manor, gazing out on to June's beautifully landscaped garden and paddocks, talking in our own special way. We spent many fulfilled hours reminiscing about our past, telling each other all the adventures we'd had since parting. The one thing that baffled me was how Cobweb had managed to retain his original name after all these years, especially when I thought back to the variety of names I'd picked up during my career. It all became clear when Cobweb explained what had happened to him since the outbreak of the Great War.

As Grace told us, he had been taken away by one of the grooms. She had been about to leave Kilwick to marry Archie Smyth and desperately wanted her beloved horse with her in her new home. Her father had chastised her and told her he hated sentimentality. What did a grown woman want with a toy horse anyway? War was declared and everyone was in a panic, trying to flee London. Unbeknown to Grace, her father had already promised Cobweb to Grace's younger cousins. She had watched as the groom had carried him down from the attic, loaded him on the back of a cart and driven off. Not knowing what became of him had haunted her for years.

Cobweb's story then took an exciting turn. The groom's wife was a Nanny to this wealthy branch of the family. The cousins' father, Lord Humbleton, worked for the Government as the Commissioner of a province in British India. When war loomed, he decided to leave Britain, taking all his family with him on his foreign posting. They had left on a passage to India from Tilbury Docks to Bombay aboard a luxurious P&O steamer ship. The journey had taken three fascinating weeks, during which they had broken journey at exotic ports. Cobweb had then spent the next five years in India with the lovely Humbleton children, enjoying a pampered life in a huge mansion on a tea plantation. After the war, they had all returned to their country seat in Gloucestershire. When Grace's cousins had grown up and married, being a treasured family member, Cobweb had been kept on for the next generation of children. But he had never forgotten Grace. He told me that when a child really needed a rocking horse as a friend, a never-ending bond was formed. Cobweb had always felt very protective towards Grace and had never stopped worrying about her. He had never felt the same about his other children, although he'd been fond of them.

Eventually, the large country house was sold when the remaining Humbletons had emigrated for good. After living with them for over 50 years and with the Kilwicks before that, Cobweb found himself at an auction house in London. Like me, he'd felt scared and lonely when circumstances had forced his family to let him go. Luckily for him, having been in the same hands for so long, his provenance, including his name and even his original bill of sale were all documented. He proved to be a popular lot and sold well, straight into the hands of June.

Cobweb went on to say he immediately felt safe and appreciated by his latest owner and he instantly liked Jacs, who appeared often to visit her friend. He overheard them talking and knew she'd been pining for a fairground horse she'd ridden as a child. How shocked he was when I told him it had been me! Our lives had gone in such different directions and our experiences had varied greatly, yet here we were 68 years later side by side. It was almost impossible to believe. Both of us knew the most important thing now, was that

Grace should be told that her nursery horse had survived and was waiting for her to see him again.

"The most priceless antiques one can collect are old friends."

Everything now hinged on Cobweb's name coming to light. June had always referred to him as 'her fellow at home' and Grace always found it painful to mention him by name; therefore no-one had made the connection. There was one man who might remember. I thought back to my days at Oil Drum Alley, when Grace first saw me in the stalls. She had told Manfri and Sinni that I was her brother's horse and that hers was called Cobweb. Surely he would remember, he'd even remarked that it was a beautiful name for a dappled grey horse. Manfri needed to know that June's horse was called Cobweb; after all, it wasn't an every-day sort of name.

I wondered if I still had my strange powers of thought. It had only ever worked on Sinni and Manfri but I was sure it could work with Jacs too; we were on the same wavelength. Cobweb was excited beyond words. All his life he had dreamed of meeting Grace again and he egged me on to try my best. So I did what I'd done in the past and fixed my thoughts on Manfri's handsome face all that day. I willed my Jacs to talk to him and mention Cobweb. Did it work? It may have been coincidence, but I don't believe in them, as you know.

That evening Manfri telephoned Jacs and we sneakily eavesdropped with anticipation. He told her he'd suddenly wondered how 'his liddle hoss' had settled in and if she was still delighted to have me with her. Clever Jacs! Almost as if she was reading off a script I'd written for her, she gushed that she was so very happy, especially as I now had a friend; I seemed to have palled up with June's horse, Cobweb. There had been a silence at the other end of the line. "Did ya say Cobweb? T'is a rare sort a name, that. I reckon that were the name o Grace's 'liddle hoss when she were a young'un."

Our plan had been successful, and events escalated from there. June was asked to find the papers from the sale and she dug out the relevant history of her purchase. The family name of Humbleton, Cobweb's last owners, was mentioned carefully to Grace during another phone call, just to make sure before breaking the news to her. Yes, she confirmed, the Humbletons were her mother's side of the family, but why the question? When Manfri told her the connection and that her precious Cobweb now lived a mere ten miles away from her, she was so amazed that she could hardly speak for the lump in her throat.

As Archie Smyth was now frail and in poor health, Grace rarely left the house. She had cared for him diligently over the years. On this occasion, Ethel offered to look after Archie so Grace could be taken to see her old nursery rocking horse, her dearest childhood friend. People can't always understand the bond that grows between a toy horse and a child. It is often the case that a loved rocking horse was the best friend a child had growing up, a secret-keeper, a giver of comfort and security. Whether the childhood was happy or sad, that horse often became very important to its owner. Some continued to be thought of as family members, even in adulthood. And so it was for Grace.

CHAPTER 14. B.L.I.T.Z.

The wonderful day came when Grace was reunited with Cobweb after so many long years of missing him. I'll leave you to imagine the joy of that meeting. Suffice to say, for the second time in my life, I felt that strange dampness in the corners of my glass eyes.

CHAPTER 15 CHARLOTTE

"There is nothing like a dream to create the future."
– Victor Hugo.

1973

Five years has elapsed since I went home with lovely Jacs, the girl of my dreams. A lot has changed since those early days. Back then we shared June's home, Wick House, with her and her husband David, their dogs and of course my soulmate Cobweb. The two Js were young, successful racehorse breeders. Their animals were reared in the stables and paddocks of June's Wick Stud. This was a part of the huge family estate, Holmwood Wick. June and her husband had created a lovely home boasting sophisticated decor and an enviable collection of antiques. We rocking horses fitted in perfectly of course! Elegant greyhounds lounged in the house or cavorted in the garden. Through the French windows, Cobweb and I could feast our eyes on the lively thoroughbred youngsters galloping playfully in paddocks beyond the garden. This was a million miles away from Oil Drum Alley or Mauler's winter quarters. Cobweb had certainly landed on his hooves here, but beautiful homes like this were all he'd ever known.

June and Jacs had worked with horses all their lives. They had joined forces some years previously with excellent results, producing many winners. Eddie had come to play a large part in this venture, working tirelessly with the girls on the stud. Life was extremely busy and everyone threw themselves into their roles of running the business. As they were all firm friends, it was a happy and harmonious home. Their evenings were often spent with us horses in the front room where we would listen with interest as they discussed future plans or recent triumphs. Often, they would eat a meal together before Eddie headed back to Epsom.

Of course the romance between my beautiful Jacs and Eddie had blossomed, culminating in them getting married in 1972. The wedding was held on June the 6th, the date of my 'new' birthday. No one could be sure of the exact day I had come into this world, but it was established that as I'd arrived 'as new' at Kilwick in 1900, I was the grand age of 72 that year. It was decided that June 6th would mark the day I was 'reborn', when my restoration had been completed. This was also the auspicious date that my racehorse double, Airborne, had won the 1946 Derby.

One of Eddie's most treasured possessions was the old plaque mounted with Airborne's racing plate from the day he'd won. When Jack Killadee died, he'd bequeathed the Derby plaque to his head man Bert Yates. Bert in turn made sure his jockey grandson, of whom he was so proud, inherited the special plaque. Eddie felt his life had changed since receiving that lucky Airborne memento. He'd met and fallen in love with Jacs and his career had taken off when he became a partner in the new business. So now, you can understand why the couple chose to marry on the auspicious date of June 6th. What a memorable occasion it was. One of those few days I'll remember for ever.

Not a huge affair, but with the most select group of people present, it was very special. I was delighted to see many dear faces from my past. Ethel, the proud mother of the groom, couldn't have been happier at the match. Manfri and Sinni attended, but Roybin was unable to come due to work commitments at Mauler's fair. With a promise to visit as soon as the summer season was over, his absence was excused. Sinni's son was keen to meet me and get to know all the people who were so important to his mother and uncle. Throughout his childhood, he'd heard many tales about us. Somehow, Roybin was wrapped up in my story and although as a child he'd never had a rocking horse, he'd grown up with Hovis, which made me feel close to him. Like a lot of my old friends, Hovis had since sadly departed.

Unfortunately, Brenda was another who couldn't make the day but had sent the couple an intriguing wedding present. Grace Smyth was determined to come to the wedding. Since Archie had passed, Grace now lived with her daughter Izzy, Alec and granddaughter Mirabel, Eddie's childhood companion. Nowadays, Mirabel also worked on the stud as a very capable head groom for the brood mares. Wick Stud seemed to connect all the people I cared about. Goodness, it really did make me feel my age, though. I had known Grace as a little girl, then Izzy and Ethel, their children Mirabel and

Eddie, who was now about to marry Jacs. It was incredible and I felt proud that I had brought all these people together and created a family of sorts for Cobweb and myself.

The marriage took place in the nearby church within the village of Wick and on that day, my Jacs became Mrs Jacqueline Marland. Have you ever known of a wedding attended by a rocking horse? Well, imagine TWO featuring proudly in all the photos, accompanied by several greyhound family members to boot! A lovely reception was held back at Wick Stud where everyone gathered to celebrate. With glorious weather, the French windows were flung open for the guests to enjoy a splendid 'al fresco' feast laid out over tables on the lawn. From our position by the windows, Cobweb and I gazed at that garden scene knowing we would hold this memory in our hearts forever. With the people we loved all around us, it was the future we had both dreamed about.

"Friends give us gifts in the hope of bringing us pleasure."

Before the couple took their leave to depart on their honeymoon, they decided to open their wedding presents so they could thank the people concerned before going away. There were many beautiful gifts but three were of great importance. The first was a huge surprise and came from June's parents. They were so fond of Jacs, who was as good as a sister to June and like a second daughter to them. They had also come to realise that Eddie was a lovely young man and the perfect husband for Jacs. Their amazing wedding present to the couple was an envelope containing the deeds to a little lodge house on the edge of the estate. Admittedly it had been empty for many years and needed a lot of work doing to it, but it would be lovely to see it lived in once again. The building was so pretty and had its own Victorian walled garden and a tiny orchard. June's parents felt it was a crying shame for it to be lying vacant. Jacs had passed this run-down lodge countless times while working at the stud as it was only a few hundred yards from Wick House. Often she had gazed longingly at the place, day-dreaming how wonderful it would be to turn it into a home for her, Eddie and me. The newly-weds were speechless. June's parents waived any thanks, saying they would discuss the serious caveats that went with it at a later date.

The second gift was presented to the pair by Manfri and Sinni. Manfri had kept an ancient milk churn he'd picked up many years before, whilst totting. He had dug out this attractive relic and commissioned his sister to decorate it in her own personal barge art style. Jacs hurriedly tore off the paper wrapping and an audible gasp was uttered by everyone. There stood the churn, upon it a stunning, colourful painting of a rocking horse surrounded by flowers – it was undoubtedly ME!

The other present of note was from Brenda. Everybody crowded round to get a glimpse of the mysteriously-shaped object. Watching Grace's face carefully, I'm sure she guessed the content. The strange package was unwrapped to reveal a beautifully handwoven child's basket seat for a rocking horse. I knew it would be perfect for me to wear. Bow-mounted horses could have baskets attached to either ends of their rockers but as I was on a swing stand, this one was different. Fashioned out of willow, it was custom made to be strapped to my saddle. With its rounded back and sides and two holes for chubby little legs to dangle through, it enabled a baby to enjoy a safe rock. There was nothing I wanted more than to once again teach a babe to ride! Grace smiled knowingly and told everyone that many years ago, I'd worn one very similar to give Izzy rides. Jacs loved it but giggled coyly saying, "Give us a chance!" Everyone roared with laughter and after all the congratulations and farewells, they ushered the newly-weds out to their waiting vehicle.

On their return at the end of the month, work started in earnest on renovating the Lodge. I was very excited about moving into what I felt could now truly be a home for life. June's parents had explained the legalities of the deal. The property was being given to them in perpetuity for the duration of their lives if they wished to remain there, with clauses they must agree to. If they wanted to move, they must hand the deeds back so the Lodge always remained within the estate. This seemed a fantastic offer and was accepted gratefully, with solicitors finalising the paperwork. Once this was done, Eddie, Jacs and I truly felt this was our new home. When not at work, the two of them could always be found at the Lodge, labouring inside and out. With the help of local builders, new lead was placed around the chimneys, slipping clay roof tiles secured, guttering fixed and all the window frames painted. Jacs worked tirelessly, clearing and weeding the sweet cottage garden and discovered an ancient herringbone brick path winding from front to back.

"A house is made of bricks and beams. A home is made of hopes and dreams."

Eddie felt his life had changed since receiving that Airborne memento.

Next, the inside was tackled. With all the walls re-plastered and decoration completed, it was nearly ready for habitation. Early in November, the couple opened the heavy oak front door and stepped inside their beautiful first home together. As they stood in the hall, Eddie declared he had a final job to do, the last finishing touch. He dragged Jacs out again to stand in the porch, telling her to shut her eyes. She heard a package being ripped open and then the hammering of nails. When she was instructed to open her eyes, she saw a smart slate nameplate deeply engraved with white lettering which read AIRBORNE LODGE. Jacs was thrilled with the new name chosen to christen the Lodge but Eddie had an even better surprise waiting. From a deep pocket he produced a beautiful replica of the original Airborne plaque that his Grandfather had left him. It was hand-crafted by the estate's talented blacksmith and was a perfect copy. This was then attached to the ancient oak door, above the heavy knocker and just under the nameplate.

Soon it was time for me to be transported to Airborne Lodge along with the last of the furniture. During the transition of moving, Jacs and Eddie had been returning to their new home late every evening but spending their days and eating meals with June. After all, there was no great hurry or deadline and the houses were only two hundred yards apart. Although looking forward to the move, the thought of leaving Cobweb behind had been playing on my mind, but I needn't have worried. I overheard June tell Jacs that all her decorating enthusiasm had rubbed off and spurred June into thinking she should give her Wick House a brand new make-over. "Cobbers will get ruined here with paint and stuff and it's a shame to split the pair up, they look so good together. Any chance you could fit him in with Blitziboy at the Lodge, while I decorate?" The nicknames June had given us made us giggle; they were a bit crass but we knew they were only terms of endearment. It was great news though, it meant we weren't going to be separated just yet, a stay of execution.

The day of the move came. The two of us arrived at the refurbished property on the back of the stud's pick-up van. We had heard all about this wonderful place but still, we couldn't believe our eyes. Airborne Lodge was even prettier than Grace and Archie's old residence, Brambler Cottage in Hidley. This was a smaller vernacular building with true cottage appeal. Cobweb spotted the chimneys before I did. They were a rich terracotta red and swirled skywards like sticks of twisted barley sugar. In a strange way, they reminded me of my golden fairground pole. The Lodge, built of local flint and brick, was tile-hung from the eves to halfway down its walls and sat under a steep clay-tiled roof. Typically Victorian in style, the barge boards were highly decorative and scalloped, similar to the rounded weatherboards above my old roundabout. Built in the shape of a cross, there were two huge rooms downstairs, each with a deep bay and two smaller rooms housing a washroom and scullery. The four small upstairs rooms had windows protruding from the eaves with their own little roofs. This lodge boasted spectacular windows throughout. These were a rare and unusual feature. They were laced with diamond-shaped iron work, each diamond holding an individual glass pane. It was delightful, the quaintest place I had ever seen.

Cobweb, more used to living in huge mansions, was struck by its cosy dimensions and asked tentatively if there would be room enough inside for us to stay together. "For someone with rather large ears, I'm surprised you didn't hear Jacs say that the parlour was very roomy, enough for the two of us, despite your huge bows!" I teased. We were taken indoors and placed diagonally side by side, with our noses nearly touching. We still had a great view out of the large bay window on to a magical old orchard. Gnarled and aged fruit trees, a mixture of pear and plum stood in the tiny overgrown patch. Next to this was clearly a once productive little vegetable plot plus a small lawned area. Half of the garden looked hacked and yellowed where Jacs had made good progress scything brambles and seeded grasses. The whole garden was surrounded by an ancient flint-knapped wall. Indoors, we both felt snug and warm despite the fire having not yet been lit. When I spied the thickness of the walls, I was not surprised. This little house already had the warm atmosphere of a welcoming home. I just knew we would all be content living here.

At the end of November we had a surprise visitor. A knock on the oak front door revealed the grinning face of Manfri's nephew, Roybin. He'd smiled with pleasure as he'd approached the Lodge and seen his mother's artistic milk churn which stood proudly on the porch and the historic adornments on the front door. As he was on a month's break from the fair, he'd offered his labouring services to the stud. It had been decided he should be a guest at Airborne Lodge during his stay. He'd also promised to lend a hand working on the Lodge's garden. His arrival was greeted with much enthusiasm. Although Eddie and Jacs had formed a great friendship with him through many phone calls, the three had never actually met yet as Roybin had been unable to attend their wedding.

I instinctively liked this cheerful, happy-go-lucky character who reminded me of a young and jolly version of his uncle. Of course, I felt indebted to him for recognising me from my roundabout days and for his part in locating me afterwards. The couple showed him into their best room and he made a bee-line for us standing in the bay. "Cobweb and Blitz, I reckon. An' more lovely than wot I thought, despite Ma and me Uncle raving on about them. Cor, Blitz was quite famous at Maulers. Nelson's old granddad has passed on now, but he never stopped going on about this little chap." As his strong, warm hand stroked me appreciatively, the gesture reminded me of Nelson. My thoughts drifted back to my fairground boy and of course my dear, clever old pal Diesel. I knew cats could live for a very long time but I was sure my poor friend would have died by now. I'd never stopped thinking about him and his extraordinary knowledge.

Jacs took Roybin's rucksack and invited him to sit while she made tea. He stood awkwardly, looking rather sheepish. We all noticed a wriggling lump moving about on his chest under his heavy donkey jacket. "Whatever is that!?" asked Jacs. With a lopsided smile, Roybin replied, "Actually, it's your belated wedding present…IF you'll have him?" He undid his middle button and the cheekiest little pink-nosed, green-eyed ginger head poked out inquisitively. Oh my goodness, this tiny face looked familiar. Making his bid for freedom, the kitten took his chance and exploded from Roybin's jacket like a rocket. Next, he darted round that room several times before alighting neatly on my saddle and proceeded to wash his face. This was how our long and lovely friendship began.

Roybin explained that Mr Mauler's son Davey had a very special cat who had died a couple of years ago at the grand old age of 22 years. Keeping useful working cats was an old Mauler tradition and they were essential for the business of pest-controlling around the winter quarters. Davey was upset at losing Diesel, but managed to keep back a 'lookalike' ginger female kitten from a litter born earlier, one of his last ever daughters. She was aptly named Marmalade and was an excellent mouser. Recently she'd given birth to seven black and white kittens and one ginger and white boy, who Davey said was the spit image of his favourite old cat. Roybin took over the care of Diesel's little grandson who had been living with him for two months. He explained that like a lot of Romany folk, he was always on the move and it was not fair on the kitten. His plan was to offer this bundle of fun to the couple as a working 'yard cat'. "Don't all stables need a cat?" he asked hopefully. Everyone agreed and was happy at this arrangement, so the little chap stayed and was given the job title of 'head mouser' for house and yard.

Aptly named Fireworks, the kitten certainly was a lively character. I very quickly realised that he had inherited Diesel's cleverness. The first time he met Eddie's lurcher dog, there had been a few tense moments. The hound had eyed him up suspiciously and made the mistake of a predatory lunge towards him. The fearless kitten had lived up to his name and instead of running, did an unprecedented thing. He leapt upon the lurcher's back as if he were riding a circus horse, claws gripping into the panic-stricken dog's neck. The pair set off round and round the room like a Catherine wheel. From sheer terror the lurcher eventually flopped to the ground, beaten. Diesel's cheeky grandson casually hopped off the poor dog and onto my saddle, looking very smug. He was never bothered by any of the stud's canines ever again.

That enjoyable month passed all too quickly and it was time for Roybin to head back to the Forest to spend Christmas with his family. His work had been much appreciated by all. Fences and buildings had been repaired and the Lodge's garden had been tidied up and landscaped back to its former glory. June tried to persuade Roybin to stay on as a full-time handyman but he'd winked in the manner of his uncle and said he never stayed anywhere for too long. Before he departed, he picked up his kitten and whispered, "You've landed on your paws, mate. It's 'cat heaven' here, so behave yourself!" With a wave and a cheery "Be seeing ya!" he was gone.

Three lovely things happened in the January of 1973. The most wonderful of these was Jac's secret news. As with most secrets, I was told first. No one other than her had ridden me since my roundabout days. I think the twins in London had only ever sat on me twice during the ten years I was with them. Brenda had assured Jacs that as she was so petite and lightly built, riding me would be absolutely fine. No other adult was allowed this privilege, which she guarded jealously.

Jacs and I enjoyed our rocks together most evenings and our magical connection was as strong as ever when she was on my back. One evening, she leaned forwards and whispered in my ear, "Soon I may be too heavy to ride you, Blitz. I may have to get that basket seat out and give it a dust." I knew straight away what she meant and was filled with joy at her news that she was 'with child'. I'm showing my age now as that was what we used to say in the old days. She was expecting her first born child and I was delighted. Cobweb must have overheard but being a wise old boy, he would adhere to the rocking horse code of preserving secrets. We could be trusted to keep this exciting news to ourselves, but Jacs wasn't the only one to have a new glow about her.

The second bit of lovely news was something all studs welcomed. Two beautiful strong foals were born, a colt and a filly, but these were slightly different to any born on the stud so far. The women were thrilled that both were born a very dark grey; from experience they knew these two would turn out to be stunning dapple greys. The colt's mother was the stud's founder brood mare Flora, a pale dappled grey. The filly was sired by a striking iron grey stallion. This was important as greys cannot be produced unless at least one parent is this colour. The foals needed to be registered and the three partners decided to give them very special names. The filly foal was christened 'Cobweb's Grace' and the colt was called 'Blitziboy', June's nickname for me. Grace was delighted when she heard. It certainly was an honour to have racehorses named after us. We felt so proud and looked forward to following the youngsters' careers.

The other event that caused a stir of excitement was June's intriguing news. She announced she'd indulged herself and bought a very interesting antique. Because the decorating at Wick House was now completed, Cobweb and I were worried. We were anticipating the dreaded day when he would be taken back to live with June and David again. One morning, June and Jacs sat next to us at the Lodge, having a quick coffee break after work. June had her arm resting affectionately on Cobweb's quarters as she remarked, "I really do miss old Cobbers, but let's leave him here a bit longer until she arrives. She's huge actually, so I need to see how she'll fit into the space." We glanced at one another and with ears eagerly pricked, we listened to the revelation that followed.

June continued to tell Jacs all about her new acquisition. She'd been trawling through adverts in the local paper and spotted a country house clearance sale. June and David had gone along to find a few pieces for their house. They were told to wander round and report back if anything caught their eye. Whilst perusing upstairs, June had seen a door standing ajar and on entering the room, she was faced with a wonderful sight. There stood a very ancient and dilapidated rocking horse. It was bald, with cracks and breaks visible, an eye and an ear missing and the deeply arched bows it stood upon were riddled with woodworm. But it was love at first sight. All June saw was its wonderful stance, fine legs stretched elegantly in the old-fashioned 'galloping' position. The good glass eye was bold and bright and held June entranced. The one remaining ear was delicately pricked atop a beautifully carved feminine head, held higher than our collected head carriage, muzzle extended as if racing. With the graceful neck of a swan and the body of a thoroughbred, this was one of the most stunning rocking horses June had ever seen. Best of all, under worn cream paint there were the faintest traces of original dapples. That apparently clinched it. She was having that horse by hook or by crook. June added peevishly, "You know me, Jacs, I'm usually so sensible. I've always said 'Let your eye be your guide, let your pocket be your judge and let your money be the last thing you part with'. Well, I'm afraid all that went out the window…" Before she'd even gone in search of the vendor to haggle the price down, she'd already named her…Charlotte.

"Charlotte?" Jacs enquired.

"Yes, you remember, from our favourite book when we were kids. The spider who saved the pig by writing messages in her web!"

"Oh yes, of course, E. B. White's book 'Charlotte's Web'. It's the most perfect name!" her friend replied.

Then we heard them discuss the details of Charlotte's restoration. June had shipped her straight down to Brenda's Dorset farm and was being briefed weekly on her progress. When Brenda had first seen June's latest buy she had been very enthusiastic and complimentary, saying she was a wonderful, rare specimen and would be a pleasure to work on. Restoration was going well and a beautifully revitalised Charlotte was expected to arrive home at the end of February. Oh, it was so exciting to think we would soon be joined by an aristocratic lady rocking horse. We just knew she'd be like us and we'd be able to converse with her for hours. What intriguing stories could this venerable old lady have in store for us? Something troubled us though. When and how would we ever get to meet? Would Charlotte be at June's, living on her own or would Cobweb be taken back to his old house to live with her? If that was the case, I'd be left by myself at the Lodge. That thought made me feel rather lonely. As is the lot of us rocking horses, we'd just have to be patient and wait to see what the future had in store.

CHAPTER 16 SEBASTIAN

1980

Time has galloped on in the seven years since I described how I ended up in the happiest of homes. Well, everything has turned out perfectly and long may it continue. My dear friend Cobweb and I weren't separated permanently as we'd feared, as the two Js found a workable compromise for our living arrangements. It was quite inspired actually, we simply moved about from home to home. After all, it was only a minute's drive between Wick House and the Lodge. If June's place was full for any reason or she and David went away, Cobweb came back to stay with Jacs and me. If Eddie and Jacs needed more space due to guests or if work was being done on the Lodge, I would be shipped off to June's. This was a lovely opportunity to spend time with the wonderful Charlotte, or The Duchess as June had nicknamed her when she'd returned from Dorset. Due to her size, she always stayed at the larger house.

Oh, Charlotte was everything we'd hoped she'd be and more. She was simply the most beautiful rocking horse we'd ever seen. At first, we were both in awe of that grand old lady and we probably had a bit of a crush on her, to be honest. She was so imposing, standing a good hand (which is four inches in horse terms) higher than us and had such regal bearing that we were slightly intimidated. As soon as we got to know her though, we realised she had a kind and wise disposition. Her many tales, told in a style reminiscent of a past age, had us totally enthralled. Charlotte had travelled extensively during her long life. Like Cobweb, she'd spent some years in India with her family during the time of the British Raj. Being looked after by Indian ayahs (nannies), cooks and many servants, she and the children had enjoyed all the privileges of a prestigious family living in India. Cobweb had loved reminiscing with her, but he'd never seen the exciting things the Duchess had witnessed.

I'll tell you one story we heard about her time in India. It concerned the various entertainers who were invited into their mosaic-floored mansion, street performers employed to keep the children amused. There was the 'sapera', a traditional snake charmer with his cobra coiled within a basket. He would open the lid among gasps of excited anticipation and play upon his flute. The snake would emerge and sway about in a trance as if dancing, which amazed the children who would be fearfully clutching on to Charlotte for comfort. She confided that actually, snakes are deaf, but their eyes would follow the flute's movements. Then there were the monkey charmers, 'bandar' men whose tiny pet monkeys would perform all sorts of tricks. The children absolutely adored these funny creatures and they'd sit astride her with a monkey perched on their laps. Magicians would use Charlotte in the repertoire of tricks they'd perform for her beloved children. It sounded as though she'd been so loved and treasured. She had been like a surrogate parent to them as they rarely saw their Mama and Papa.

Charlotte had enjoyed a long and varied career working in many illustrious places. She'd modelled saddlery and racehorse clothing, had famous children sit on her in a photographic studio while their portraits were taken and once, she'd even featured in a well-known movie film. Having been with several wealthy families all her life, it came as a dreadful shock, as it did to us all, when WW2 broke out and her latest family fled from their ancestral home, leaving her behind. Before they left, the estate gardeners had carried her to an air raid shelter within the grounds, where she'd spent most of her war years. That was probably the reason for her sad state of physical decline. Decades later, when the empty old country house acquired new occupants, she'd been discovered by workmen and transferred back into the dilapidated mansion, to be sold off with other unwanted items. This is where June stepped into Charlotte's life, discovering and rescuing her. She described herself as having been in a 'tatterdemalion' state, a word we had never heard before and had no clue to its meaning. Like me, she was taken to Brenda to be re-born and returned looking more stunning than June had dared to hope. Charlotte was a totally fascinating character with the most perfect manners. Although we were rather shy at first, she encouraged us to tell her our own life stories and always listened with genuine interest.

After conversations with The Duchess, we often found ourselves trying to fathom the meaning of words she'd used in her strange flowery way. There was one that had us completely baffled. Young Fireworks always came to the rescue and provided an answer. He had inherited his grandfather Diesel's clever and curious ways and had a particular penchant for words. He could be very annoying, but I loved the little chap and on this occasion he proved helpful, if a bit over-zealous. On hearing our dilemma, he'd leapt into my saddle and sat bolt upright with his little chin raised up as he recited his answer. "Tatterdemalion; an adjective meaning scruffy, tatty, run-down, decrepit, care-worn, threadbare, seen better days, derelict, rag..."

"SHUT UP, Fireworks!" – we both screamed in unison. He looked surprised and hurt and started washing his face furiously.

I said gently, "We get the picture, but you do go on a bit. Charlotte's often said 'the young feline appears to have ingested an encyclopaedic tome'. What's that mean then, clever clogs?"

This diffused the tension and we all had a good laugh. Fireworks chuckled, "She's right, I've swallowed a dictionary!"

"True integrity will never be compromised."

Now, here's the last intriguing thing to tell you about Charlotte. She was very 'old school' and strict about the rocking horse code of keeping secrets and guarding keepsakes. She said integrity and discretion were our middle names. When Brenda had worked on her restoration, something precious had been discovered within her belly. This 'something' was handed over to June, a tiny sealed vial-like container made of opalescent mother-of-pearl. It was very beautiful and exquisitely made. No one could guess at its contents, but it had to be something of great importance to someone, judging by its fabulous container. Cobweb and I had heard about the mystery object whilst eavesdropping on the two Js when they were deep in conversation at the Lodge. After much discussion, June had decided not to open the fascinating iridescent vial and had concluded that 'maybe secrets were best left as exactly that'. She planned to replace it into Charlotte's belly for safe-keeping. We were eaten up with curiosity and when the opportunity arose, we asked The Duchess if she knew what was inside the treasure. Her answer was that of course she had 'intimate and absolute knowledge of the esteemed contents'. Our huge school-boy mistake was trying to push her into disclosing what she knew. Those beautiful shining glass eyes turned on us and gave us a look that nearly scorched the dapples off our backs!

"The most precious necklace you'll ever wear are the arms of a much-loved child."

I've left telling you about the best bit till last, because the coming of Sebastian has completed my happiness and rounded off my story up to now. I still adore little Jacs but I have a new love in my life, Eddie and Jacs' little son. Sebastian Bertram Marland was born on July 3rd, 1973. His arrival couldn't have brought more joy into our already happy home. In the early days when he was a tiny baby, Jacs was very preoccupied with his care and I spent a month with my friends at June's house. Cobweb and Charlotte were just as excited as I was and quite envious that I had a new child in my life. On arriving home, I had the pleasure of giving baby Seb his first taste of riding. From then on he rode me constantly, first in the basket seat but soon progressing to saddle and neck-strap.

Let me explain quickly about neck-straps, hopefully without boring you. They are an essential piece of kit when learning to ride. This is a loosely-fitted narrow leather band which is fitted around the base of the neck. When held, it encourages riders to keep their hands low. It is also something to grab hold of if needed, rather than using the reins attached to our mouths. A jab in the mouth is most unpleasant for all horses and in my case, 'heavy hands' over the years eventually caused my weakened jaw to fracture and break during a bumpy van journey. Damaged bottom jaws are a common injury inflicted on us poor rocking horses. Un-schooled children always pulled hard on our mouths either for balance or to make us rock faster, and this is so wrong. Pulling heavily on reins should never be employed when riding any horse, but I never blamed the children as they simply hadn't been taught to have 'sympathetic hands'.

Sebastian's loving father was the wisest of teachers. He doted on his son and gave him time and attention. As soon as Seb was old enough to sit in my saddle unaided, Eddie tucked my reins away and replaced them with a loosely fitting neck-strap as the one I wore on my traditional harness was too close to my neck. He encouraged Seb to ride using only his natural balance, with the neck-strap there for grabbing in emergencies. Jacs would often come into the room and scold gently saying, "You two, make sure you look after my son. Don't you dare let him fall." The toddler was taught how to get me moving by using his weight, or gently pushing on my neck, when he was really small. Eddie made riding me as much fun as he could.

Seb adored me and every day would ask excitedly if he could ride 'Bliss' (he couldn't pronounce Blitz). Each exercise was treated as a game and the hours we spent together 'play riding' reminded me of my years in Newmarket teaching those little apprentices. Seb was better than any of them by the age of five. He had natural talent, impeccable balance and the lightest 'seat', which describes the effortless way in which he sat correctly. Eddie then promoted Seb to using 'cotton reins'. He threaded sewing cotton through the rings of the metal bit in my mouth and the lad had to ride me using only this thread as reins. It was a challenge set by this father; rocking me without ever pulling on my mouth. Never once did he snap that thread. By the age of six, Seb and I had an unbreakable bond similar to the bond I felt with Jacs; he rode me as if we were merged together as one and you can imagine the make-believe races we won together! The little lad was so light that he was given the nursery nickname of Shuttlecock. Oh, how I loved my little Shuttlecock. With his arms around my neck, whispering my special name, 'Bliss', in my ears, my contentment was complete.

Saddle me, shoe me and send me a horse,
With a dear little bit and a bridle, of course.
With real little stirrups to put on my feet,
A real little rocking horse, racehorse complete.

(Doll Child Poem C1900)

These valuable early lessons were the making of Sebastian. He became the loveliest rider I'd ever had upon my back. He was a wonderful child in every way. I loved Sebastian deeply and not only when he was riding me. He, Fireworks and I could just be together for hours, enjoying each other's company in amicable silence in the parlour at the Lodge. Other times, we would discuss words that Seb had heard during his day. The 'walking dictionary' cat was always there with an answer. The little boy saw us for who we truly were, he had that rare quality of insight. Seb and I were able to communicate in a way I had not encountered before, even more intensely than I could with Jacs. Maybe it was because he was still a small child and of course, he had a very special mother. I'm sure his riding skill came from his father who was a talented jockey, because good riders are born, not made. As you read this, Seb is seven years old and I am surrounded by a loving family, wonderful friends and a life I could only have dreamed was possible. My story is coming to an end, but I'll let you into a secret. Later in his life, Sebastian entered into the racing industry; he very soon became a champion apprentice and then a leading top jockey. I'm not surprised, but very proud to have had a hand in his schooling.

What of my other dear friends? Of course, some of the older folk have now sadly departed but new generations are coming along. Ethel adores her little star of a grandson and Izzy and Alec are the proud grandparents of Mirabel's first child. Manfri and Sinni visit often, bringing Roybin along whenever he has time off. He eventually married into the Mauler family and now has a beautiful wife, one of Davey's daughters.

The stud is flourishing, and those two special foals grew up to be successful racehorses. 'Cobweb's Grace' won five valuable races and retired to join the other brood mares at Wick stud. Her first filly foal born earlier this year has been named 'Graceful Charlotte', and guess what colour she is? Yes, she will be a dappled grey. Hopefully she will be a winner and go on to breed her own foals which will continue the trend for years to come. The only mystery that I can't enlighten you about is the unanswered question which still intrigues Cobweb and me. What was in that secret vial found in Charlotte's belly? That is for the Duchess to know and us to guess.

Did you ever wonder what became of Manfri's idea, the notion of writing down my life story? Well, you are reading it right now. It's taken years and a lot of collaboration between everybody who remembered me, going back to Nelson's grandfather who knew my Maker, Wilf. Grace, who is now a serene great grandmother of 86 years old, is as sharp as a pin and she put everything for the story into some sort of order. She remembered many details from Kilwick Manor and the Rectory. Grace, Manfri and Sinni have known me the longest and had a huge part to play in my tale. Izzy and Alec too, put down many early memories and anecdotes. That fateful day I met and fell in love with Jacs was the day that shaped the rest of my life. The pain of losing her for all those years has now been rewarded. I owe my present happiness to Manfri, June and Jacs, who went the extra mile to find and rescue me, with the help of Brenda of course. She gave me back my body.

It took a special person to be able to write about my strange, long life, someone who truly knew my inner thoughts, fears, hopes and dreams. Although everyone helped with their pictures and memories, it was of course my wonderful Jacs who has put the words from my heart on to paper. However, my life isn't over yet and it's a sad fact that we rocking horses can live a lot longer than the people we love. I'm old and wise now, so I've accepted this truth. That's why family is so important. If, like me, you didn't have any to begin with, gather the people you love around you and make yourself a family, as I have. I know I'm extremely lucky to have my heart. I know I'm blessed to have found a safe haven and I sense that Sebastian will always be my soulmate and guardian. He will be my future.

The End

A wise old rocking horse lived with his folk,
The more he saw, the less he spoke.
The less he spoke, the more he heard of course,
I wish I could be like that wise old rocking horse!

Printed in Great Britain
by Amazon